Shadow of the Beast

Twisted Dark

Anna M.L. Koski

ISBN

SHADOW OF THE BEAST

This book is a work of fiction and any reference to real historical events, people, locations are used fictitiously. Other names, characters, places, and incidents are the product of the author's imagination and any resemblance to actual events or places or persons, living or dead, is purely coincidental.

Also available in eBook.

Cover Image by Unsplash, Wil Stewart (Unsplash)

Cover Design by *The Round Table*

To my readers

Y'all are the best.

Seriously.

Also, Aunty, if you read this book

No you didn't.

Warning of Coven Thirteen

To those who seek
A place without eyes,
With dungeons so deep,
That echo with cries.

Coven Thirteen
Is where you must go
But keep your hands clean
No crimes you must show

For if your soul is not pure
And you pass through the walls
Endless torment you will endure
As your screams echo in empty halls

Wary to those who seek
The walls of scorn
For they also speak
You have been warned

~

Prisoner's warning of Coven Thirteen
Jail of Witches
Beholden to the Warden
Elder Witch Irma

Violent Violet

I don't need magick to kick your fucking ass.

~

Violet

Magickless Witch

Indentured Slaved

KIDNAPPED

Chapter One
Gold Coins

"One thousand eight hundred and thirty-three." I sighed out the number, setting my last gold coin on its stack. The brilliant yellow of the gold coins always made me feel better and if I needed to feel better its was now. I still hadn't quite recovered from Florence's... *visit.* A phantom pain ran over my nerves and I shivered at the memory of claws slowly moving through my flesh as the vicious witch had asked me the same questions again and again.

Where were the two werewolves? '*What werewolves?"* hadn't been acceptable.

Who were they with? '*I don't know.*' hadn't been acceptable.

Do you know where they went? '*I don't understand.*' hadn't been acceptable either.

It took me two long and drawn out deaths before I had finally cracked. I blinked back tears at that. I cursed the very day I was born and handed off to the brutality of Elder Irma. I shifted my left foot, the thin chain locked around my ankle forever reminding me of my position. I had no clue how Florence had learned of the time check spell on the chain and I had a sneaking suspicion it had been Irma who had told her.

I wasn't a fucking idiot, the *very* last witch I wanted to piss off was Miranda Lenkirion but I could only take being killed and regenerated so many times before my fear of it happening again overrode my fear of the powerful witch. The fucking time check *curse* on my chain meant that I could be killed but I wouldn't stay dead. I would be back in the land of the living when the time check spell lost my pulse. It reversed the damage and brought me back to the point of when the spell was last activated and it was activated daily.

It was like I was stuck in a form of hellish stasis. Dying was a *horrible* thing to endure and I had endured it a lot. It was why the gold was so comforting to me. I was trying to get enough gold to buy my freedom from Elder Irma. I had no clue what the debt I owed was but gold was hard to come by and I had gotten a significant amount of it. Nearly two thousand coins was a very generous amount and it was hard earned. I had to deal with illegal potions out of the back door of the shop to gather my gold. Elder Irma didn't pay me, slaves didn't get paid.

I shoved the thought away. I *would* pay for my freedom and I *would* be free of the chain on my ankle. I just needed to sell a few more potions and I would have over two thousand gold coins. I knew that Elder Irma would have a hard time refusing that size of payment. I just hoped it was tempting enough for her to accept it and let me go.

I took care of the shop for her but since I had grown up she hadn't used me for her experiments. I was thankful for that, *very* thankful for that, but I just wanted to be free.

I let out a small sigh as picked up my coin bag, slowly putting stacks of coins into it. I hadn't been allowed to practice my magick, hadn't been allowed to test for my levels. I had looked at the world around me through a cage my entire life. I just wanted to experience *something* without a chain rubbing my ankle raw.

I managed to clear the table of my coins and I closed the bag, trying it shut. It felt a bit heavier and I could hear the coins clinking around in the velvet. It had an ever space spell on it. I could put as much stuff as I wanted into and it wouldn't weigh too much or become full. I had managed to get it as a trade for a wellness potion I had created that created the illusion of youth and vitality. It was time and effort well spent in my opinion.

I stood up from my spot at the back table before I walked towards my corner I did my best to ignore the faint sound of the tiny chain moving along the floorboards behind me. It just reminded me of my place, as did my corner. A tiny, lumpy mattress on a rope bed frame ticked between several barrels was where I called home. I knelt down and shoved at one of the wooden boards of the barrel closest to my bed. The piece shifted inwards and I wiggled the bag into place before pushing against the metal band of the barrel, popping the panel back into place.

I stood up, brushing my dusty hands off on my light dress. I knew I was being overly paranoid because Elder Irma never came around but I still didn't want to take any chances on anyone finding it. It paid to be paranoid, I knew that very well.

I could hear the chime of the bell as the front door to the shop opened and I moved towards the warped mirror that stood over a rusty water basin and I smoothed down my hair, forcing a smile onto my face. There was no need for anyone to tell the Elder witch I wasn't being nice. She didn't come around but I also knew the witch never passed up on an opportunity to punish me.

I moved towards the front of the store, leaving the back quickly. The chain around my ankle became lighter and harder to see at the presence of another person around. Another little perk of the fucking chain, no one really knew it was there and I couldn't say anything about it or why I had it. Elder Irma didn't particularly like sharing and I knew that she knew that the spells on the chain made me a very special case if someone wanted to use me to get at her. That was probably also why I had no clue where Coven Thirteen was. The Elder witch was paranoid to a fault.

I tucked my hair behind my ears and once again pasted the smile on my face as I came around the front desk. "Welcome to the Broken Crow. How may I help you?" My voice trailed off as I blinked at the large form that nearly took up the entire doorway. I slowly looked up, my eyes following up the chest to a thick neck, that held several tattoos and a strong jaw and severely set mouth.

A glint of gold caught my attention as I spotted several small hoops rested along the male's ear lobe. My throat grew dry as I finally met the male's gaze. His eyes were a rather startling blue as they looked around the shop and his lips curled up into what looked like a snarl and his white teeth glinted against his tanned skin.

The apparent and rather dangerous aura that hung off of him had my eyes widening and my heart racing with fear even before his eyes gleamed with a hint of ferality and a growl rumbled his chest.

A fucking *werewolf.*

I felt like my heart would escape my chest as I looked at the dangerous creature that had just decided to drop in. The last two times a werewolf had been in my shop something very bad had happened to me and I didn't think this time would be third time's the charm.

Chapter Two
All That Glitters

The scent of dust assaulted my senses. Mold was a close second but the scent of the witch I wanted was no where to be found.

Find her

My instinct sliced at my nerves, its rage present in my bones and skin. It urged me to rage, to let the beast loose to tear and kill till we found the witch who had stolen from us. I fought the urge off. I needed to be smart, the witch didn't play fair so I couldn't play by normal rules.

I slowly looked around, taking in the cluttered shelves and the dusty air. I narrowed my eyes, grinding my teeth together as a growl rumbled my chest. The witch wasn't there but I knew this was her shop. The fae I had grabbed and tortured had told me as much. I gave the room once more scan before my eyes landed on a pixie like face.

I jolted slightly, surprised by the small female. Her eyes were wide and I could practically taste the fear that radiated off of her but I couldn't help how my mouth tugged up. If the little pixie worked in the witch's shop, then the little pixie would know where the witch was. I started towards her and she inhaled quickly, her eyes growing wider before she let out a small chirp of fear before turning and bolting.

I curled my lip up in agitation before I followed her, my long strides eating up the distance between us and I caught her around the waist right as she entered the back room. She let out a piercing cry of fear that had me wincing but I ignored it as I set her down.

"Sit." I pointed to a barrel and the little witchling looked at me, her fear thick in the air around her. I narrowed my eyes as I moved closer. "*Sit.*" Her form trembled but she didn't move, her eyes still terrified and locked on me. I let out a snarl and grabbed her around the waist, setting her on the barrel, ignoring how she gave another sharp cry.

"Be *quiet!*" I snapped the words out, unable to take anymore of her piercing sounds against my sensitive ears. "Where is the witch?" I spat the words out but her mouth stayed firmly shut as she trembled, watching me as a doe would have my beast, frozen in terror of the death to come.

Make her talk

Need to find witch

My instinct was relentless but even I had a line. I wouldn't needlessly harm a female, certainly not one as pretty as the little pixie. Females were delicate creatures, needing to be protected, not tortured. Besides I knew with how scared she was she would tell me anything I wanted to hear, true or not, if she was even able to speak at all. Not to mention the sour stench of fear that hung off her. She was useless as she was.

I pointed at her, narrowing my eyes as claws wanted to push out of my nail beds. "Stay." I bit off the word, daring her to defy me as I moved back out to the front of the shop. The bitch had to have some sort of clue as to where she was hiding. I needed to find her, she needed to die. No one took my brother without paying for it. I had been tracking her for weeks, ever since she had snagged Lyxton from our northern camp. I wasn't going to simply give up my twin without a fight.

I bared my teeth before starting to turn the place over, looking for anything that would help me find the witch or her coven. I didn't care about the breaking glass or the items I destroyed as I cleared shelves in my search. It served the bitch right. I narrowed my eyes, my anger hot and burning on my tongue. It had only grown since Lyxton had been taken. Each day he was gone it burned brighter, grew hotter. I knew it would only disappear when the witch was dead by my hands. The bitch would pay for messing with my blood.

I moved to the front desk, yanking at the drawers, searching through the papers for something I could use. There was nothing but meticulously written receipts and precisely placed pens. I dumped the drawers out, heedless of their well placed contents as I knocked on the bottoms, searching for a hidden compartment somewhere.

I tossed them away with disgust as each drawer gave me nothing. I stalked back into the back room, the little pixie still sitting on the barrel, her eyes wide and the fear still hanging around her. I was surprised she stayed or hadn't attempted to retaliate against me. Witches were notoriously vengeful when they wanted to be, the End Bringer has shown us that much.

I started pulling lids off barrels and slats off crates, digging around in the contents in my search. I was becoming increasingly agitated as my instinct hissed words at me. I kept glancing at the little witchling, knowing that I could hurt her just a little and she would sing for me but I continually pushed the thoughts back. Lyxton would fight me to the bitter end if he knew I had mistreated a female in my rescue of him. Witch or not, he was the gentleman of us two. I always found his manner to be boring and too human like but he was my twin and we held a strong bond and I loved him regardless of how he chose to act.

I grabbed a barrel and the little female made a small eep and I snapped my head to look at her. Her gaze was fully on the barrel, her small hands grasping at the edge of her spot so tightly I could see her knuckles turn white. I narrowed my eyes at her as I made a fist and slammed it down on the top of the barrel, splintering the wood. She made another sound and it made me more determined to get to the contents to the barrel. To my surprise it was empty except for a purple velvet bag at the bottom.

I picked it up, it had a slight weight and when I jiggled it I could hear numerous coins clicking together. The soft patter of bare feet on wood was all the warning I had before a dainty hand tried to snatch the bag away. I immediately lifted it up above my head as the witch jumped for it, an angry sound in her throat. She made another jump for it and I watched her carefully. There was no fear to her, only vexation.

Opportunity arises

Take it

My instinct settled down and I jiggled the bag, making the coins click together. The witch's eyebrows drew together and anger made her face flush slightly as she looked at me, her jaw settling itself in a stubborn position.

"Give it back." It was a harsh demand carried in on soft tones and I suddenly understood what my instinct was telling me. The little pixie would do much for her gold coins, even give up the Elder Witch who had Lyxton.

"Such a wee thing ye are but I'll give it back if ye can take it." I slowly lowered the bag and she jumped for it again, an angry cry in her mouth as I yanked it out of her reach. I repeated it until she refused to jump again. "Can't, can ye?" I watched as the angry red grew darker on her skin as she glowered up at me, all fear gone.

I bent down closer to her, enjoying the anger she showed, the *defiance*, because I knew I would stamp it out. "Tell ye what. Take me t' the witch an' ye'll get yer gold back." I wanted to smirk at her, the little witchling would have to make a deal with the devil to get her gold back and she didn't know this devil would burn her master's world to the ground for the evil she had done to me and mine.

Chapter Three
Brute Force

I stared up at the male, glancing between him and my bag of gold. I wanted to hit him, do something, *anything*, to get him to let go of what would buy my freedom.

"What witch do you want?" Not that I could help him anyway, I was stuck and couldn't lead him anywhere even if I wanted too but he didn't know that.

He lowered the bag slightly as he stared at me with those clear and burning blue eyes. "Ye know which magickal bitch I'm talkin' about." The bag lowered a fraction and I snagged my hand out but he yanked it back just as quickly, my fingertips just brushing the velvet. I let out a sound of frustration as his mouth curled upwards. "Ye ain't gettin' yer gold until I get my witch." He held the bag above his head, his knuckles almost brushing the wooden beams of the shop's roof.

I glowered at him, huffing slightly. "I *don't know* which one you are talking about." I crossed my arms over my chest. The werewolf was just a vexing as Miranda. I had no clue why people liked to play mind games with me. I didn't see what appealed to them about it. It was frustrating.

His chest rumbled darkly, reminding me of just what I was glaring at, "I have ways of makin' ye talk, pixie, ye don't wan' me t' use 'em." It was a thick warning, his accent growing stronger as his rumbling increased.

I swallowed hard and slowly took a half step back, needing the space between us so the fear wouldn't overwhelm me. "Contrary to popular opinion, us witches don't just know each other. You need to be more specific." I didn't like the tone in his voice, it made my skin crawl, reminded me of another werewolf who made me talk. I slowly rubbed at my arms, backing up further. I *never* wanted to endure that again.

"It's clear ye do, pixie." He gave a harsh gesture to the room we stood in. "Yer workin' for her." At that, my face paled and I felt like my knees had turned to jello. He wanted Elder Irma. He moved closer, nearly looming over me as he bared his teeth, the golden glint of the gold in his ears and the white gleam of his teeth dividing my attention as the rest of his form seemed to darken around me. "I wan' the witch. Yer gunna take me t' her."

I felt like I was prey underneath his gaze and I swallowed hard before attempting to steel my shot nerves. I just was not comfortable with such a dangerous creature so close to me. Especially not after the last one. My eyes darted to the table where Florence had tied me down so her werewolf could torment me at his leisure. I felt my hands slowly start to shake as the fear soured in my stomach.

"Ye are gunna help me, pixie, one way or another." The tones were low and ominous and I snapped my gaze back up to him. My mind raced with how I could tell him that I was incapable of leaving the shop and couldn't actually tell him where Irma was.

"This might be hard to believe." I gave another swallow, my throat dry with fear. "But I don't know exactly where she is." I watched as his eyes narrowed and I shifted on my feet, getting ready to bolt. I knew that look, Florence's werewolf had that look before he had used his claws on me. He took another step and I flinched downwards, almost huddling into myself. "Please do not hurt me!" I couldn't help the terrified words that came out, my heart beating in my ears as I practically cowered on the floor.

He immediately backed up, his eyebrows furrowed as he looked at me. "I ain't gunna hurt ye, pixie." His voice was low and gruff as he stared. I felt my cheeks heat up as I slowly stood up, moving another step back from him. I didn't want to be in the same room as him, not with that fucking table. I glanced at it and back to him. I could just imagine him pining me down and his claws digging deep into my flesh. Bile rose up and touched the back of my throat at the memory of just that.

"I doono what ye are thinkin', pixie, but ye look sick." He said it evenly and I swallowed hard, pressing a hand to my mouth hard as if that would stop the rolling of my stomach. "Yer gold for the witch. Tha's all I want." He jiggled the bag again and I shook my head.

I couldn't explain about the chain or the spells and I didn't dare take my hand away from my mouth. I was afraid that I would throw up if I did so. I didn't want that, to be covered in vomit before he mutilated me. My heart thumped unpleasantly hard in my chest as the space seemed to grow smaller, my skull squeezing.

"Jus' take me t' her." His voice was a low rumble that seemed to ripple the air between us and I blinked up at him before my hand dropped. I felt very faint.

"I can't." Stuck once again but this time I couldn't tell my potential tormentor the answers to his questions. I would be mutilated and tortured and wouldn't have anyway to stop it.

"Ye can." At that I just shook my head, looking at the floor before I pressed a hand to my forehead, cursing myself. I should have been stronger, should have been able to look him in the eyes and tell him to fuck off but I couldn't bear the thought of being killed like that again. I *never* wanted to die by another werewolf's hands ever again.

"Fuck this." His voice was a sharp sounding weapon and before I could dart away he grabbed me around the waist and carted me out of the backroom. "Ain't gunna take me t' her, I'll draw her t' me." I struggled against his grip, my breaths coming in violent pants as I tried to escape.

I looked up and realized the door had come into view and I braced myself right as my chain was pulled tight around my ankle and I was yanked back. I bit back a yelp of pain as it dug into me as he gave another tug, looking down at me with confusion. He grabbed me tighter and gave a steady pull that had another cry of pain escaping me from the chain nearly cutting into my flesh before I reached up and managed to slap his ear.

"Fucking *stop*!" He immediately dropped me and I scooted backwards, lifting up my skirt slightly to rub at my sore ankle, the skin raw and marked but not broken. I was thankful for that. Those wounds took a very long time to heal.

I became aware the werewolf had crouched right beside me. I froze, nearly turtling as he reached around me, his hand grabbing my ankle before his thick and rough fingers moved against the chain, the contact making me jump. He made a noise in his throat before he found the line of chain.

He looked between me and it. "Ye can't leave, can ye?" The question was simple and anger flared up brightly in me.

"That's pretty fucking obvious, isn't it?" I grabbed the chain and gave it a hard yank as if to punctuate my statement. I glared up at him. "Instead you had to try and caveman me out of here and that fucking *hurt*. This shit is like razor wi-" My throat immediately constricted, sending me into a violent coughing fit that had me gasping for air. I cursed the spells on the chain repeatedly as the feeling subsided and I felt like I could breathe.

When I looked around the werewolf was moving towards the backroom, his hand following the chain. I stood up on slightly shaky legs and dusted myself off angrily. I was *not* having a good week.

I followed the werewolf as he reached where the chain was attached to the floor, he gave it an experimental tug. The chain looked like a gossamer spider web strand, delicate and fragile but I knew just how strong it was. He gave it another tug, tilting his head as he looked at it.

"That's not going to work, its spelled down." I got the words out right before that crushing force squeezed my throat again, sending me into another coughing fit.

It cleared up and I blinked rapidly, wiping at my red face as I looked at the werewolf who was looking down at the stone where the chain was before he moved to the side and gave one heavy tug. The chain didn't budge. I slowly sat down on a barrel as I watched him ineffectively try to remove the chain from the stone. He tried numerous different ways to pull it and nothing seemed to work as he grunted as he exerted quite a bit of exertion to break the chain.

I thought he was giving up as he rolled his head on his shoulders make his muscles bulge before slowly wrapping the chain around his hand, bringing it closer to the floor. I watched, waiting for the chain to cut into his skin as he slowly pulled upwards, his neck and face turning red from the exertion. I knew he wasn't getting anywhere but then suddenly the chain flickered, going from the thin gossamer to the darker steel before flicking back. He gave another grunt, baring his teeth and my eyes widened as the chain flickered again and there was a small crack and the magick gave way, leaving him to tear the chain from the stone floor.

My mouth dropped open as he slowly unwrapped the chain from his hand, looking completely unbothered as he stretched the marked up appendage. "Magick doesn't beat brute force, pixie." He slowly looked at me and I blinked at the chain. My heart thudded in my chest before I glanced back up at him. My chain was free and the werewolf was the one who did it. I swallowed as I slowly stood up. There was only one reason the werewolf freed me and I *knew* I wasn't going to like it.

So I bolted for the exit.

Chapter Four
Short Leash

I narrowed my eyes, inhaling the crisp forest scent deep into my lungs. Frustration filled my bones as my instinct crawled through me. It had settled down with the little witchling, no longer wishing for me to harm her to get the words from her. The plan to use her as bait for the witch seemed a better alternative. It would draw the witch onto the territory of our choosing, take her out of her element.

I glanced over my shoulder at the little witchling that stuck close behind me, her expressive brown eyes warily glancing around at the forest we were walking in. She was a strange little creature. Had fought me *hard* as I pulled her out of the shop, doing her best to escape but the moment she had exited it and realized we were no longer there, she had damn near clung to me instead.

The little pixie seemed *terrified* of the outside world. I wasn't used to witches, they rarely came to the Northern Forests but I knew that they weren't timid little mice like this little pixie was.

However, despite how scared she seemed to be I also knew it could be a trap. I knew witches were deceitful. It was how the witch had taken my brother. Rage burned at my gut, chewing on my spin as my instinct rolled through me like a freight train.

Find female

Kill her

I tightened my hand around the thin chain in my fist as I gritted my teeth together. We *would* find the witch and she *would* die. I also knew that with the little pixie it would be that much easier. I didn't doubt for a moment that an Elder witch would come to the rescue of such a fine and dainty female. Especially one that had been taken by a werewolf. The witch would be coming to find me the moment she realized her trapped little pixie was taken from her cage.

I could hear the sound of a flock of birds bursting from a bush further away and I lazily turned my head towards it while the little witchling inhaled deeply, nearly pressing herself to my back.

"What was that?" It was a terrified little voice that came from her and I shrugged, only slightly curious as to just how well she managed to play the terrified little female. I wondered just how much it pained her to press close to the creature that had so terrified her before.

Her fear had been thick and sour and her face had continually paled and on one occasion she looked like she would be sick. Yet she stood behind me, a hair's breath from touching me, acting as if everything around her was absolutely more terrifying than I was.

I picked up my speed, needing space away form her before my instinct turned on her once more. It would demand answers as to why she switched so quickly, why she went from being terrified of me to pressing close as if for protection. I wasn't in the mood to harm a female, no matter what my instinct said. I glanced over my shoulder once more and the little witch stumbled as she walked, wincing as her bare feet stepped on the debris that littered the forest floor.

I slowly raised my eyebrow at her lack of shoes. I turned away, the silly female should have been wearing them. It was not my fault she would get hurt because of it.

"Where are we going?" There was an almost breathless tone to her voice, as if she had exerted herself too much and I shrugged.

"Must keep movin', pixie." I couldn't stay in one place for too long, the Southern Forests and the Northern Forests didn't always get along. The Southern Forests were closer to the Covens and I didn't need another set of witches after me for taking the little pixie. I was setting a trap and I didn't need to catch any wayward witches within it. I was after only *one* witch, one that I would destroy completely and totally.

I was used to the pace I set, my brother and I were nomads, we followed the hunts, only staying in cabins when the northern weather turned for the worst. It made me curl my lip up more at the thought of the Southern werewolves, they were pampered, so used to having their food handed to them that they no longer knew how to hunt, how to survive. They were spoiled whelps and it was no wonder the witch went after my brother and I. We were both in peak physical shape, we were both at our most virile.

Lyxton and I had discussed females before he had been taken. I knew it was time for us to find suitable breeders but there were very few pickings for that.

Fae were not compatible for offspring, humans were but the birth killed the breeder and the shift would kill the child. It was best not to endure such pain and so we avoided them completely.

We had both decided we would require female-weres. I knew would be difficult to find one but I also knew that with time we would have found at least two we could protect and keep happy. After all female-weres chose their males based on heritage and strength. Nothing that Lyxton and I lacked. Any breeder I would have taken would be pampered. It was what they deserved for creating life.

Find witch

My instinct hissed it at me, its agitation once again rolling through me, punishing me for not listening. It did not understand plans. It relied on actions of my own, not the actions of others. There was a curse from the witchling and when I glanced over my shoulder she was limping, glowering darkly at nothing in particular before she looked up at me, as if sensing my gaze on her.

"Can we stop?" There was a faint edge of pleading to her voice and I shook my head, despite the faint pang within me that the poor female was delicate and was more than likely not used to the punishing pace I had set out on.

"Keep movin', pixie." At my words there was a muffled angry sound from her that had my mouth twitching. I wasn't sure if it was to smile or to frown. For such a timid thing she had a mouth.

"Asshole." The spat out word had me stopping and I turned around, looking at the small witch. She glared at me, her expression dark with anger.

"Pardon, pixie?" I moved closer and she glowered back at me, her jaw set in a position that told me all to well she had deliberately said it loud enough for me to hear.

"I don't have shoes, you forcing me to walk anyway makes you an *asshole.*" She looked more than vexed with me as she gestured at her feet, wincing as she shifted on them. "I just want to go back to the shop! I have *nothing* to do with any of this." I looked her up and down, only half listening to her. She had a nice form, thinner than most but I could tell that she had the curves required to make a male want her.

I slowly walked around her, letting the chain dangle from my hand as I did so. "Ye help me, pixie, ye get yer gold an' I get my witch." When I once again in front of her I yanked my hand back, the chain catching the back of her free ankle and sending her crashing to ground with a small, surprised cry. I crouched down beside her as she sputtered, sitting up with a dark look on her face just barely covering a wince.

I held the thin chain up, could feel the magick thrumming through it as she glanced at it and then back to me. "I hold *this*, pixie, *don't* ye forget it. What I say goes." I stood back up. "Get up, we need t' keep movin'." I turned around, not waiting for her as I started walking away.

I had no time for idle chit-chat, no time to speak or wait for delicate females to keep the pace. I felt slightly bad for it but there was little I wanted to do to rectify it. The witch had my brother and I wanted him back. The little witchling was just a means to an end.

There was no tugging from the chain, letting me know she was once again walking.

"She won't come for me, you know." Her words were clipped and I shook my head.

"Pretty witchlin' like ye bein' taken by a werewolf will have tha' witch up in arms." It was one thing I knew for certain. Witches did not like werewolves taking other witches. Besides I stole her from the dusty shop, breaking the magick that bound her there. Taking someone's slave would be enough to piss off anyone.

"You are *naive.*" The witchling stressed the word, derision coating her tone thickly and I whirled around, pointing at her as I snapped my teeth together.

"Say *one* more word, pixie." I glared at her, daring her to push me more. My instinct still wanted her tormented and tortured for information and I wasn't above doing as it asked.

"Its *Violet.*" She glared right back at me and I rolled my head on my shoulder.

Punish female

My instinct started pushing at me hard and I tightened my hands into fists, claws pressing into my flesh. "Ye are testin' patience I doona have." I watched as her defiance slowly disappeared, her disgruntled and vexed edges disappearing as she once again turned into that timid mouse.

"Why do you care so much about Irma anyway?" She muttered the words glancing at me but no longer glaring her fear slowly growing, slowly wafting off of her.

I scanned her face, faintly appreciating the beauty it held. She was a finely made female. "Goin' t' kill her." I turned around, once more moving through the trees, the little witchling following me like a dog on a leash. "Goin' t' kill the bitch." I snapped my teeth together at the thought of the witch's throat between my jaws. How I would *enjoy* ending her life.

Chapter Five
Night Terrors

The trees were towering over me, I had never thought they would be so big. Stories and pictures would only show you so much but this was beyond my imagining. I felt stupid and idiotic but they... scared me. I had never seen one in person before and if it wasn't for the throbbing and aching pain in my feet I knew I would have been utterly terrified.

There was a tug against my ankle as the werewolf yanked on my chain. I bit back a whimper as I tried walk faster. I felt hot and sweaty and horrible. I just wanted to go back to the shop. The Forest wasn't welcoming, everything felt hostile. It was absolutely strange to me but the broad back of the werewolf tugging me along like a little puppy felt like the safest thing around me.

He was literally the only thing that was familiar and that I was fairly certain he wasn't going to kill me, hurt me maybe, but not kill. I had no clue about anything else that was out there, as far as I knew everything around me currently wanted me dead.

I limped along behind him, biting my tongue to keep from asking him to stop. Each time I had done so he had always responded with a gruff no. My legs were almost numb but my feet felt raw and searing. I just wanted my stupid and shitty bed back in the shop.

I stared at the ground, my bottom lip quivering. I pushed my sweaty and limp hair back from my face. I wanted to be brave and put a strong face on but I was painfully aware I was a witch without the use of my magick and I was in a world I did not know or had been prepared for. I was at the full entire mercy of whoever held my chain.

It was getting darker and much harder for me to see. I was barely even aware when I stepped on anything because my feet hurt so much anyway that all the pain just seemed to all blend together. I just wanted to stop, I had never walked this far or moved this fast my entire life. I was exhausted, in pain, and just wanted to go home. It was shitty and terrible but it was better than where I was currently.

The pace was far too punishing and my legs wobbled as I tried to keep up. My feet felt like they were on fire and my bottom lip trembled. I bit it to keep it from being too obvious. I took another step, my hand against the rough bark of a tree to steady myself, and my legs buckled. The chain immediately went taut, my leg was jerked, and I was nearly dragged. I yelped and the werewolf whirled around, glowering at me.

"Get up." It was a harshly said command and I just stared at the ground in defeat.

I expected him to retaliate but there was a still silence in the air before he moved towards me. I flinched as he drew closer but he didn't touch me, merely wrapped the chain around the tree, tying it in a complicated knot that made my head hurt to watch. He said nothing as he moved away. I brought my knees up to my chest and leaned against the tree, feeling drained and weak.

I tried my hardest to not focus on the vast wilderness I found myself in. How I knew I couldn't escape because of the chain tied tightly around my ankle and the tree. The thoughts of the danger I found myself in were invasive and made my head and chest ache unbearably. I had been scared of Irma and the things she would do to me but it was a different sort of fear that now clung to me. The feeling of uncertainty, of feeling as though you were suddenly very tiny underneath the vastness of the things that surrounded you.

Everything was so big out in the world, even the werewolf was almost uncomfortably large. I could see his form was coiled thickly with muscles as he moved around, his expression fixed into a severe glower as he kicked rocks towards trees, clearing sticks and debris from a rather large area on the ground. The muscles rippled across his form, straining against his shirt, his longer hair pulled into a hair tie at the nape of his neck. I could occasionally see the feral gleam in his eyes and the glint of the gold he had in his one ear. My gaze drifted to his neck where I could see the tattoos, dark against his skin. I wondered what types he had, *how* he managed to get them, werewolves healed rather quickly.

He turned towards me and my eyes flicked to his face right as he glanced at me, meeting my eyes. I felt frozen underneath the blue of his gaze, his eyebrows lowered and a rumble escaped him. "What ye lookin' at, pixie?" It was a harshly said question and he seemed to make himself taller, puffing out his chest. I swallowed but couldn't find my voice as I looked at his large and intimidating form. "Ye gunna tell me?" He took a step forward and I looked down at the ground, trying to gather myself so I could respond. I couldn't do that when his gaze pierced into me, straight through my body and to my very core. It made me very uncomfortable, as if he could see everything about me with that azure gaze.

It took a moment and I gave another swallow before glancing up at him, avoiding his eyes, my gaze falling to his strong jaw. "You're really big." I felt stupid the moment the words came out and my cheeks flushed bright red and I immediately lowered my gaze, wrapping my arms around my knees.

I could hear him approaching and I stared hard at the ground, at the dark of the earth that was littered with pine needles and leaves. He crouched in front of me, I could see his large hands as he rested his wrists on his knees. "Aye, I am big... an' yer small." He reached for me and I couldn't help how I flinched slightly but it didn't seem to deter him as he pressed a knuckle underneath my chin, gently moving it upwards until I met his gaze.

He looked my face over, that piercing gaze seeming to burn over my skin as he traced my features. "Wee little pixie, ye are." His voice was low and it rolled across my skin, making a heat coat my neck and cheeks. "Pretty thing... dainty.... *delicate.*" His voice lowered another octave and the rolling turned to a distinct rumble over my skin.

He brushed his thumb across my lower lip and the contact made me inhale quickly. It was a sharp heat and the volatile sensation was slightly foreign.

"Ye are built t' make a male beg, aren't ye?" He let out a chuckle before removing his hand and standing up, towering over me. "Get some sleep, pixie. Ye need it." He moved away, going to the spot he had cleared before laying down.

My bottom lip still burned and tingled from the contact and I pressed my fingertips to it, wondering how he had caused such an immediate and visceral reaction within me. My feet giving a sudden throb distracted me and I gave a small whimper as I tried to adjust them so they weren't pressed hard against the ground. I shifted, leaning against the tree as I wrapped my arms around myself, trying to stay warm.

I gave a little shiver as the darkness of night made the air drop from cool to cold. My dress was torn and flimsy and within a few moments I felt cold right down to my bones. I clenched my teeth to prevent them from clattering together in my mouth, I shivered uncontrollably and closed my eyes tightly. I was exhausted but the pain in my feet and the cold kept me hovering on the very edge of the sleep I so desperately needed.

It was a haze where I was aware of myself but nearly asleep, unable to pass through to the peace and serenity that beckoned me so sweetly. A heavy crack of a tree branch had my eyes snapping open and I sucked in a breath at the oppressive darkness that enveloped me. My heart thudded in my chest as I strained to hear what was out there and another cracking sound was heard in the same direction, directly behind me and the tree.

Fear made my mouth go dry and I scrambled across the ground, reaching for the werewolf. The chain stopped me ten feet from him and I bit my lip to keep from screaming. I could hear a faint huffing sound from behind me and I turned quickly so I was sitting, staring frantically into the dark, trying to see what it was that seemed to be right there. I felt like I was being watched and when I twisted to look at the werewolf my hand landed on a decently sized rock. I picked it up and threw it at him. It thumped off his back and my heart thudded in my chest hard as he sat up, turning his head. The gleam of his eyes were bright in the dark as he let out a heavy growl, those gleaming eyes narrowing at me.

"There's something here." It came out in a choked whisper and I could hear the huffing growing louder behind me and the feeling of being watched like prey grew. The werewolf crouched, narrowing his eyes before he slowly advanced towards me. His gaze was on something over my shoulder and it made the panic ratchet up even worse in my chest. I hadn't been imagining things. There *was* something behind me.

When he reached me one large hand grasped my shoulder and pushed me down gently. "Stay down, pixie. Doona move." His voice was a low rumble and I nodded, curling in on myself on the ground. The chain was pulled tight but I ignored it, shuddering in my ball as my breathing came in frantic pants that bordered on sobs. My heart thudded almost painfully in my chest and there was a heavy growl before the sound of something crashing through the bushes had me curling tighter into myself.

There was a shout and a squeal before a snarl rattled the air out in the trees. I jumped at another squeal before a heavy thud of something hit the ground several feet away from me. I flinched and fought the instinct to bolt, the werewolf had told me to stay and he knew more about the Forests than I did.

If he said for me to stay down then there was a reason for it.

The thing that hit the ground grunted before shifting in the dirt. "Fookin' pig bastard." The words were snarled and when there was another squeal the werewolf let out a heavy growl and moved away. I lifted my head slightly, looking into the direction where I had heard him go but there was nothing but darkness. I could hear the squealing move further away and the sound of something heavy crashing through the brush before the sounds were immediately cut off.

The silence seemed more disturbing than the noises and I tucked my head back down, my breathing coming in pants as I tried to listen for something, anything, that would be coming towards me. My heartbeat counted the seconds that passed, the pounding seeming to get harsh and more painful with each moment that came and went.

Without warning, the thin chain around my ankle went lax. I inhaled deeply, freezing in my spot as I tried to listen for an approach but my heartbeat seemed to override any sounds I might have heard.

Large hands grasped me and I tried to scramble away, my fear making me panic at the surprise contact, distressed and almost inhuman sounds escaping my throat as the fear tried it's best to suffocate me.

A shushing sound was all there was as the hands grasped me tighter and pulled me to a large form. I instantly turned to the werewolf, clutching at his shirt as I shook violently. I felt like I was going to be sick. The fear made bile touch the back of my throat and my form trembled uncontrollably.

"'S okay, pixie." His voice was gruff and my teeth chattered together as I clutched his shirt so tightly my fingers ached. "It's dead." There was a curious softness to his tone that I didn't have the mental capacity to think about as relief surged through me.

"Th-thank yo-you." The words were stuttered out from between my clattering teeth. I pulled myself closer to him, closer to the warmth and safety of his large form. He tensed, grabbing my wrists. "D-don't t-tie me to-to the t-tree a-again, pl-please." I hated how badly I stuttered the words out. I doubted I had ever been so scared in my entire life and I had been terrorized nearly daily for *years*.

Tears burned at my eyes as the werewolf pulled my hands away from him, the fabric of his shirt leaving my nearly numb fingers. He shifted his grip, holding my wrists together with one hand before the thin chain was wrapped tightly around my wrists. I blinked in confusion, only seeing faint movements as my eyes tried to adjust to the darkness but failed miserably.

His hand dropped from my wrists and a thick arm wrapped around my back and I was lifted off the ground, my legs dangling as the werewolf carried me several feet before setting me down, pushing me so I was laying down. I was unsure of what he was doing until he laid down behind me, snaking an arm around my waist and pulling me so I was tugged tight against his chest, his heart beating strong against my back. I felt a tiny spike of fear as his breath stirred my hair and his other arm moved underneath me to wrap around me as well.

I could shift my hands, the chain was tight but not biting around my wrists. I felt wary of having him at my back but it soon faded as the warmth of his body sunk into me and I was enveloped by a sense of security by his large form pressed against mine. He was a dangerous creature, yes, but currently he was protecting me and that was all that truly mattered when one was stuck in a world they didn't know.

I waited a bit, listening to his even breaths before I felt the courage to speak, the fear finally loosening its hold on me. "What was it?" The question came out as a whisper and there as no change in his breathing and I thought he had fallen asleep until his hand spread out over my stomach, the large appendage stretching from my navel to my sternum. I shivered underneath the touch, unsure of how to feel about it.

He gave a small grunt. "Big boar. Territorial bastard was tryin' t' scent ye out." His words did little to comfort me. Everything out in the forest *was* out to kill me.

"Thank you for killing it, werewolf." I shuddered to think about what would have happened to me if he hadn't been there, if he hadn't woken up.

"Name's Jaxton." He shifted behind me, his grip on me growing just a fraction tighter. "People call me Jax. S'ppose ye can call me tha' too." His voice was a low rumble that vibrated my back.

"Thank you, Jax." His name fell off my tongue easily and I felt my cheeks heat up at it. I felt a little embarrassed by the reaction it caused but didn't have time to ponder it too deeply as a rumble came from his chest.

"*Sleep*, pixie." His tone was all the warning I needed to keep my mouth closed and my eyes shut. I thought it would be hard to fall asleep, my distrust for the werewolf overriding my exhaustion but within a few moments of closing my eyes I was fast asleep, feeling safe and warm.

Chapter Six
Temptress

The first thing I realized when I woke up was that the little witchling had turned in my arms sometime during the night, her face nearly pressed against my chest. Her breaths were warm against my skin and her hands once again clutched at my shirt as if she was afraid I would have pulled away from her.

That lead me to my second realization, that my cock ached and twitched at the feeling of such a soft female being encased in my arms. There was no need for the little female to cling to me when her honeyed scent made me want to growl and press my face between her breasts and lavish her with my attentions until she *writhed* for me to sate her. There was no need for her to cling because I wasn't in a mood to let her go.

The thoughts were a welcome distraction for me. I hadn't had a female in a very long time and I knew this particular little female would take little to no pushing to allow me to use her as I would. I had seen the flash of desire in her eyes when I had touched her and even now I could smell the sweet scent of her desire. It was faint but it made me aware that her dreams were... *heated.*

I slid my hand down her back, palming one ass cheek and there was a faint moan from her before she pressed her face closer, nuzzling my chest, her little hands tightening on my shirt. I gave her ass cheek a small squeeze, giving a grunt as she pressed herself closer, one of her pale and shapely legs drawing up to my side.

"Temptin' pixie." I muttered the words out as I looked down at her. Her lips were parted and she rocked her hips slightly I caressed her, moving my hand from her upper back all the way down to the soft and full swell of her ass.

I wanted to sink my fingers into it as I pulled her over top of me. I wanted to grind my painful and swollen cock against her sweet smelling sex. I could imagine her pretty face flushing and her pert little mouth opening with her moans as I did so. I felt my mouth quirk upwards as I looked down, watching her rosy lips moving with her deepening breaths. Those lips begged to be kissed, to be claimed and teased until she was hazed with pleasure.

Breed female

She's receptive

My instinct curled around me and it was hard for me to push it away because with how my cock was aching, I wanted that more than my instinct did. I closed my eyes and gave another grunt as I gripped her ass tightly in my hand. I could practically feel her hot and slick pussy sliding down my cock as she pleaded with me to fuck her, to not hold back.

I had never had a witch before and I had always generally stayed away from them but as I told her last night, she was made to make a male beg. She was more tempting than the others I had come across, more fine, more delicate.

I also had come to the conclusion that the little pixie was not able to use her magick so I didn't have to worry about the thoughts that she was placing a spell on me to want her. My mind was my own when it came to my desire to fuck her.

I caressed her ass again, liking how she rocked her hips against me, although she just a touch too high to reach my cock. My instinct slowly hissed at me to take her and I fought it back. Despite how she was using me to pleasure herself, I knew that it would scare her too much to find me over top of her without warning.

The little pixie would require a little teasing until she felt confident enough to approach me. I had to make her think it was her idea to fuck me or close too. It would take me a bit to get her to trust me with her desire but it wouldn't be hard for me to do. I took it as a challenge more than anything. The little pixie had piqued my interest and she had no idea what she was in for.

She muttered something, pressing her face closer to my chest. I knew I had a few reservations about her but after last night I had no doubt that the little witchling was not acting. No one could have acted *that* fearful or *that* relieved to be safe. For some strange reason the little witching was truly scared of the Forests. I didn't particularly understand it because that amount of fear must have come from someone who had never seen the things that Forests held before.

There was a faint noise from her as her dress moved up her leg, baring one pale thigh to my view as she gave a faint grumble. Her expression turned into a small frown as her leg tightened over my side and she rocked harder against me.

It was damn near torture to feel her using me and smell her desire without being able to indulge myself. I slid my hand down from her ass to that bare thigh and a faint but happy sigh escaped her. Her skin was smooth, soft, and supple. I bit back a groan as my cock throbbed and ached. I knew that if I stayed where I was that I would end up fucking the witch.

I pulled her leg from around me and moved backwards before sitting up. I did my best to ignore the little sounds of agitation she made in her throat as I removed her hands from my shirt. As much as I wanted to bury myself deep within the witch, we needed to get moving. I looked down at the witch, scratching at my jaw. Her dress was still high up on her thighs and was twisted strangely around her chest, giving a rather nice view of the curve of the side of her breast.

I tilted my head as I looked at her. She was a fine female and the more I looked at her the more I wanted to make her moan for me. I needed to distract myself, remind myself of how much time it would take before I was allowed that so I reached over and unwrapped the chain from her wrists. She moved slightly, frowning before her eyes fluttered open. I watched as she blinked those brown eyes at me, her focus was slow coming. I waited for the fear, the apprehension, to appear but she merely closed her eyes once more, her breaths evening out.

"Pixie." I gave her shoulder a small shake but she merely made a face and muttered something underneath her breath, smacking her lips together. I raised my eyebrow and gave her another shake.

"Go 'way." One slim hand lazily waved at me as she curled up further as if trying to fall back asleep.

"Get up, pixie." I kept my tone firm before I gave her a harder shake. Her eyes popped open and she scrambled slightly, her eyes narrowing as she looked at me. I fought back a smirk at the deadly look on her face as she sat down. "We need t' keep movin'." I stood up and gazed down at her. She rubbed at her eyes and I rolled my head on my shoulders before walking away, her chain wrapped around my wrist. She would follow or I would drag her.

There was only faint tug and then the sound of her agitated muttering as we started our journey once more. She seemed to lag behind more, taking more tugging from me on her chain. She also grumbled more, muttering insults at me underneath her breath. I had to admit that was the exact reason I had to tease and torment her to get her to give into me. Despite how timid she was, when the little witch was vexed she would let you know it and not very nicely.

An hour passed before my hand was yanked backwards rather violently. I turned around to see the little witchling sitting on the ground, a dark expression on her face as she held the chain in her hand and gave it another tug.

"Get up." A dark growl rumbled my chest as I moved towards her. She looked up at me, defiance stamped across her face before the sheen of tears in her eyes stopped me in my tracks. "*Pixie.*" My voice was gruff and I looked away from her eyes, unable to see that sheen and not feel guilt clench my stomach.

"No! My feet *hurt.* I'm not walking anymore." There was the tiniest warble to her voice and I cursed myself silently as I finished my walk to her and crouched down, grasping one of her ankles. I lifted it up and looked at her feet. The bottoms were dirty but I could see the bruises and the cuts and scrapes they had on the bottom. I lightly trailed my finger down the bottom arch of her foot and she hissed. I didn't blame her, I could feel how warm it was with swelling.

"Stupid witch, should 'ave worn shoes." I set her foot down to glare at her and she glared right back, her chin going into that stubborn position before I reached out and grabbed one of her wrists with my hand. She inhaled sharply at the contact before I turned and pulled her arm over my shoulder, reaching down and grasping one of her thighs and hoisting her onto my back.

"Put me down." There was an edge of uncertainty to her voice and I shook my head, moving her higher up onto my back before I stood up. She was stiff on my back but I ignored it.

"If ye ain't walkin' then I'll carry ye." At my words her other arm slipped over my shoulder and I let her wrist go to grab her other thigh, settling her legs around my waist before I started walking once more. She was a tiny weight on me, felt like she was a slip of something nearly as light as air. It didn't matter how far I walked, she still remained light. I wondered how often she was fed to be as slim as she was and another wave of guilt rolled over me. I hadn't fed her last night and without being sure how long it was since her last meal it was no wonder she was so worn out.

I narrowed my eyes as I stroked on thigh with my fingers, adjusting her on my back. She had relaxed, her head resting on my shoulder as I walked. I would feed her, provide her with food and perhaps she would be more forthcoming with not only information but the tight little body she had. I would bury myself in her before the moon reached the end of its cycle, it was only a matter of time before I charmed my way into her bed.

A growl rumbled out of me and I tightened my grip on her soft and supple thighs. I wanted to buried deep inside of her and that want was fast turning into a need with how badly my cock ached. It also didn't help that her breasts were pressed tight against my back and her breaths brushed over my neck slowly and gently. At that I frowned before turning my head.

The little pixie was asleep, her arms danging over my chest and her face peaceful as she slept.

Good female

Trusts us

Have advantage now

My instinct was pleased with her sleeping on my back and I had to admit a faint surge of satisfaction tightened my gut as I realized just how much the little witch trusted me with that action. We were always defenceless when we slept but she hadn't even given that a thought and had merely fallen asleep, trusting me to protect her at her most vulnerable.

Easy to find witch

Female will help us

My instinct was right in its rasping tones. The more she trusted us the more we would learn of the evil bitch who had taken Lyxton. Once we knew enough we would be able to rescue him. I could only imagine how badly he was suffering at her hands. I ground my teeth together and shoved the thoughts away. Currently I had a female to cater too and I knew Lyxton would consider the slight detour of my plans a well worthy expedition. I shifted off my course, searching the ground.

If I wanted to make the female trust me I had to give her a reason to believe I wouldn't cause her anymore undue suffering and I knew in the process that she would spread those pretty and pale thighs for me. With that thought and the throbbing in my swollen shaft I redoubled my efforts to find the specific plant that would aid me along. I had a witch to catch but more importantly a pixie to convince into a hard fucking.

She gave a sleepy mumble, her hands tightening on my shirt once more as she wiggled on my back. I could feel her nipples stiffening and I grinned. With how she was acting I knew it would take me very little effort to convince her at all.

Chapter Seven
Vibrant Dreams

The world came back to me as I was set down. I wanted to blink, confused as to where I was as a large hand held the back of my head, lowering me down to the ground.

"Settle, pixie. Sleep." His voice was a low rumble and I curled up, hating that the warmth of the werewolf was now replaced with cold earth. It was uncomfortable and hard and I knew I wouldn't be able to go back to sleep now that I was awake. At least not while on the cold and hard dirt.

I rested my head on my arms, cracking my eyes open. The werewolf's back was to me, the sound of sharp clicking was all I could hear, his shoulders moving smoothly before he bent down, breathing out in a steady stream. When he shifted I could see the faint glow of the fire he had started. I shifted, sitting up and wincing at the absolute hellish stiffness my muscles had. I felt sore and my feet ached unbearably.

I rubbed at my eyes, wincing once more as I shifted in my spot.

My gaze followed the werewolf as he guided the fire to grow. He seemed intent on his task and I felt free to watch him. He was strong, that much was apparent, it thrummed through his limbs and his touch. My cheeks flushed at the reminder of how I had been pressed against that wide back and just how *good* it felt. I wiggled slightly in my spot, embarrassment coating me thickly. It wasn't that I was a prude or a virgin, I had my fair share of Fae males it was just he was a fucking *werewolf.*

Jax.

My brain supplied his name, correcting me and my cheeks flushed even worse at the sound of it. He was a rather attractive, sinfully strong werewolf named Jax. I wasn't supposed to like werewolves like *that.* It was illegal for me to even speak friendly with one. Let alone have wickedly sensual dreams about them where teeth trailed across my flesh and eyes gleamed with desire as hot hands gripped my body. I clenched my hands into fists, pressing my face into them.

The dreams had been a shock to me, something that had happened suddenly. I didn't fucking understand it. He scared me, when his intensity was shoved onto me I wanted to do nothing but hunker down and hide. The jump between fearing him and desiring him was a vast vast canyon, an impossible leap to make but a part of me wondered if it was how he protected me that created the bridge over said canyon.

He hadn't actually hurt me, yes my feet hurt and were battered to shit but he hadn't physically put a hand on me that was cruel. He hadn't even explicitly or truly threatened my physical well-being and had protected me from the boar the night before. I had only read about the animals but I didn't doubt that it was a large one. It had fucking tossed the huge werewolf. That alone let me now that it was just as oversized as everything else out here.

The fact he protected me was probably the reason he had become the main dark star of my dreams. I shivered as the images from my dreams flicked into my mind. Low rumbles moving over my skin and rough hands caressing my skin as teeth nipped at my neck. Images of my fingers tracing the dark tattoos on his neck, discovering where they lead. I felt like my face was glowing as it heated even more. It was to the point I couldn't even look at him without flushing. I stared at the ground, opening my hands and pressing them to my cheeks.

"Have a good sleep, pixie?" At the question my eyes widened and I nearly choked. I couldn't look at him after my previous train of thought. I froze slightly but I knew I had to reply so I just gave a small nod. I stared down at my feet, shifting them before reaching down and trailing my fingers over the bruised flesh. I needed something to distract me and that seemed like a good thing to distract myself with. They were sore and I could feel them throbbing. Even gently touching them was slightly painful.

"Here." I jumped when I realized Jax had come over. I looked up at him, my eyes wide. He crouched down beside me before sliding his arm underneath my knees and his other around my back before he picked me up.

I inhaled sharply as he pulled me close to his chest. "It's cold over here. Let's get ye t' the fire." His voice rumbled through his chest and into me. I looked at the side of his face, my eyes drawn to the small gold hoops that followed the shell of his ear. He carried me towards the small fire before setting me down in front of it. I felt a bit confused as he removed his arms, grasping the chain before coiling it up and leaving it beside my feet.

"Are you not going to keep hold of it?" I pointed to the chain, looking at him with a heavy bit of suspicion. He was so adamant about me being under his control because of the chain, the fact he was just leaving it was more than suspicious.

His mouth twitched upwards and his blue eyes narrowed at me with amusement. "Ye gunna run, pixie? Go ahead. I won't stop ye." He gestured with his hand towards the tall trees that surrounded us. I looked around at the darkening Forest before looking back at him. He chuckled, grinning at me, his teeth glinting. I narrowed my eyes before reaching out and shoving at his shoulder. "So violent the little Violet is." My name from his lips made me shiver and made a flash of anger roll through me as I reached over and shoved him again.

"Prick." I spat the word out, turning away from him, my face flushing.

"Aye, I *do* have one of those, pixie." His chuckle was like dark velvet and I did my best to keep my eyes from widening at his words. "If ye want... ye can touch it." There was a heated tone to his words that had me whirling to look at him, my eyes wide and my face bright red.

"Don't be *vulgar!*" I spat the words out at him. That was the *last* thing I needed him to say to me with my mind in the fucked up mess it was because now I knew I would be helpless in my dreams of what said portion of his anatomy looked like.

He reached out and chucked my chin with an amused smirk. "Yer cute, pixie, 'specially when ye blush red." He got up and moved away, leaving me to my heated cheeks and my whirling mind. I hunched forward, glowering at the fire in front of me, thankful for the heat it gave off as night slowly tried to creep its way over the Forest.

I let out a huff and Jax came over, shoving what looked to be a water filled can into the flames. I inhaled, wincing as the flames encased his hand but he merely pulled his hand away, unbothered by the fire he had literally just shoved his hand into.

"Doona look so surprised, pixie. I've got thick skin." He grinned at me again before he moved back to doing whatever it was he had been doing previously. I bit the inside of my lip, I didn't understand why he was acting the way he was. He seemed more relaxed, less severe and stern and he seemed almost... *interested* in me.

I shivered at that and wondered for a brief moment what that would be like before I mentally slapped myself silly. That was an *actual* death sentence and I knew that if I got caught I would be thrown into the fire. Unlike Jax, *I* didn't have thick skin and I wasn't keen on learning how it felt to be burned alive. I shuddered at the very thought of it, my mouth growing dry. I frowned, my mouth was dry regardless. I hadn't had a drink in over twenty four hours.

I went to stand up when Jax was back, pushing down on my shoulders sharply. I made a noise of protest when he crouched down behind me, squeezing my shoulders in his large hands. "

Doona move. Ye'll hurt yer feet more." He dropped his hands from my shoulders and went to move away when I huffed my agitation, looking over my shoulders to glower at him. "Problem, pixie?" He lifted an eyebrow as he looked at me and I gave a short nod.

"I'm *thirsty.*" I went to stand up again and he once again pushed me back down before he held a canteen right in front of me. I blinked at it as he gave it a slow shake. I could hear the water sloshing against the insides and I reached for it only to have him hold it out of my reach.

"If yer needin' somethin' ye *tell* me. Doona be a little mouse, can't take care of ye if ye are." His voice was gruff before he brought the canteen closer, letting me take it from him. I hastily opened it and greedily drank the water inside of it. It was cool and had a slightly strange taste from being in the canteen but I didn't care.

The water hit my empty stomach and I felt relief. I pulled the canteen away, wiping at my face with the back of my hand before I realized Jax was staring at me from his place beside the fire, those blue eyes hooded and reflecting the flames and making them seem sinfully heated.

I flushed and closed up the canteen, my eyes falling to the skirt of my dress. A thread of disgust moved through me at the dirty and torn fabric. I wanted to change out of it but knew I couldn't. I felt all sorts of dirty and unclean but I knew there was literally nothing I could do about it. The flames of the fire slowly started to lower and I watched as the werewolf put some sort of leaves in the can he had placed in the flames. His focus on it was intense before he shifted, grabbing the dead carcass of a rabbit he had from his other side.

My eyes locked onto it and despite how I felt a pang in my chest that the poor little bunny had died, my mouth watered as he stripped the hide off it and tied it to a stick. He held it over the flames as he put another log onto the coals.

My stomach growled loudly and he lazily looked over at me. "Sorry 'bout tha', pixie. I'm used t' goin' long times without food. Won't be long 'fore ye can have some." My stomach let out another rumble and I pressed my hand to it. I couldn't remember the last time I had a decent meal, it had been a few days. I had to live off of what I could get through trade or what Irma remembered to send to me and that was never enough.

My gaze landed on Jax as he rotated the rabbit in the flames, the scent of cooking meat filling the air. He wanted to kill her and I couldn't say I *didn't* want him to complete his goal but I also knew Irma wasn't going to come for me. She didn't care about me, she had made that perfectly clear to me as I grew up. I was an object, a *thing,* she could use whenever she pleased and she could do whatever she wished to me. It made my teeth on edge and I wanted to help him but I knew I was entirely useless to him.

"What did Irma do?" I asked it and he shifted, titling his head as he looked a the fire.

"Took my brother from camp. Tricked us both. No one does tha' t' me and mine." His voice turned guttural at the end and he looked at me, his eye gleaming with his beastly nature. "What would she be doin' t' him?" At the question I paused, looking at the flames.

"She's never taken a werewolf before." Never once in the twenty six years I had been with her had I ever remembered her taking one. It wasn't a smart move. It caused unneeded tension between the species and more scrutiny on her and Coven Thirteen. I knew that was something she didn't want. "She's always been given witches to work with. There has never been a need for her to take anyone else." There was more than enough witches for her to torment and experiment on. Her taking a werewolf made no sense.

He gave a small grunt. "Tha' why she had ye?" I could feel his eyes on me but I just stared at the flames, the brightness of them burning into my retinas.

"I don't know why I was given to her." She had simply told me my mother had dropped me off at her door, going to live in a small town far outside of Coven Thirteen called Havenbrook. I knew the exact location, the street address and house number. Everything. Just another way Irma controlled me. "I don't remember a time when I wasn't with her. She's been there as long as I can remember." Nothing but memories of her. I had no memories of my parents and at times it made me *ache*.

"Ye grew up with her." At that I gave a small shrug. I didn't really want to get into what growing up with her entailed. "Can ye tell me what she would be doin' t' my brother?" There was an edge to his voice that had me softening slightly, it was clear he missed his brother, worried for him and I felt bad that I couldn't put his fears at ease.

"I don't know. We know all we can about werewolves. Her taking him makes no sense." I gave another shrug, frowning deeply. "Experimenting on him wouldn't work for magick and she wouldn't learn anything from it that we didn't already know." I gave a heavy sigh. "Maybe she's just trying to rile things up. She's fucking crazy." The Elder witch had been left alone to experiment for far too long. I could see the slow descent into madness that she was currently on.

She had been growing more and more volatile and unpredictable. It was why I was so happy when she put me in The Broken Crow. I was far from her torment and her rages that seemed to come far too frequently.

"Tha' she is. Took my brother. No one does tha' t' me." His tone was dark and I slowly looked over at him. His expression was nearly angular and his jaw ticked with his agitation.

"She stays at Coven Thirteen but believe me when I tell you I don't know where that is." I didn't want him to hurt me thinking he could get the information.

"Why should I, pixie?" He glanced at me, lifting the rabbit out of the fire and I narrowed my eyes at him, shifting in my spot

"Because that witch has tormented me my *entire* life and I would give *anything* to see her dead." I had dreamed about it growing up, having one of her spells back fire, burning her in her workshop, having my magick come in strong and fast so I could kill her myself. I had no feeling or need to protect her. It was my fear that kept me in line but removed from her grasp I no longer felt the need to fall to her wants. "Why would I protect her from a sure fire way of making sure she couldn't hurt me anymore?" If I had the information I would have told him but I couldn't because I didn't know.

He gave a slow nod. "Fair 'nough." He used the end of the rabbit's stick to shuffle the can from the coals before setting up several rocks to hold the rabbit over the flames. "Feet." He gestured to me and I blinked at him in confusion. He glanced at me, the fire playing with the shadows of his face and the gold in his ear as he gestured to my feet.

"Feet. Let me see 'em." He held out a large hand and I frowned before shifting to tentatively stick out a foot in his direction. His warm palm grasped my heel gently and he dipped a cloth into the can, rinsing out the excess water. He looked at the bottom of my foot before moving the cloth towards me.

I jerked my foot away, wary of what he was doing but he merely looked at me. "'S okay, pixie. Jus' Comfrey an' St. John's Wart. Helps with swellin' and bruises." He grabbed my foot again, holding the heel in his hand once more as he gently smoothed the wet cloth over the bottom of my foot. I hissed slightly at the pain the action brought and he made a faint noise in his throat. "Easy, pixie." He glanced at me, his blue eyes piercing into mine. I pinched my lips together and he continued his ministrations. The herbs made my feet sting and I bit my lip, closing my eyes against the pain.

"Talk t' me, Violet." His voice was gruff and I cracked my eyes to look at him. His gaze mine captive. "Will help with the pain." My mind raced, trying to figure out a good topic to talk about as he continues with his treatment.

"Why are you being so nice?" I was suspicious of it to be honest. His shift in behaviour was concerning for me and I wanted to know why.

"Brother mainly." His gaze was intent on my foot as he dipped the cloth back in the can before returning to my foot.

"Why?" I watched him, my face twisting with pain as he moved to a new part of my foot. My foot felt like it was on fire but there was a faint numbing that was starting to move over the spots he had done.

"Kick my ass if he knew I was treatin' ye poorly." He gave a small shrug before he set my foot down and picked my other one. His fingers brushed the skin of my ankle, slipping underneath the chain around my ankle. "Why do ye have this on, pixie?" He looked up at me and I stared at him, keeping my mouth closed. "Can ye even tell me?" I looked away, hoping he would pick up on the action to mean no.

"How badly did tha' witch treat ye?" His voice was rough as he started to wipe the cloth against the bottom of my foot.

I ground my teeth together, watching him, trying to figure out how to answer the question. "Badly enough that I would tell you where she was if I knew." I tugged on my dress, hating how ragged and dirty it looked. "I know how brutal werewolves are. I wouldn't wish that on anyone but her." I looked up at him and he had stilled in his movements before those blue eyes met mine.

"Brutal, aye, tha' we are." His fingers stroked the skin of my ankle. "But anythin' I do t' ye, pixie, ye are gunna *beg* me t' do." He flashed me a grin and my cheeks immediately flared red and I looked away while he chuckled, the rich sound melting into the dark night air.

"I wouldn't beg you for anything." I muttered the words out and that rich chuckle turned into a husky laugh that rolled over my skin and heated my cheeks.

Chapter Eight
A Little Push

I shifted the little witch on my back. "So ye are tellin' me tha' ye've *never* been t' the Forests." I couldn't help the disbelief that coated my tone as she shifted her arms around my neck.

"This is my first time. I spent all my life in Coven Thirteen or the shop. I wasn't allowed outside." She shrugged, I could feel it and I was nearly blown away by it. The thought of being denied the wilderness was just *wrong.*

I couldn't understand witches. Why deny anyone the world around them? "Is tha' normal? Does tha' happen often with witches?" I had seen witches out and in the Forests so the fact the little pixie had been denied that was so absolutely strange to me.

"No." The word was sharp and I shook my head, digging my fingers into her pale legs. "Irma was... *different* in how she brought me up." The way she said it let me know she wanted to say something else but she either couldn't or just didn't have the words.

"Tha' witch..." I scowled darkly. She was already dead in my mind but I wouldn't mind drawing it out for her for her treatment for the little pixie. "I doona understand how she could do tha' t' such a dainty female." I didn't understand witches. I doubted I ever would. Who could ever look at such a delicate and small creature such as Violet and want to deny them *anything*?

A small hand clipped me upside the head. "Who are you calling *dainty*?" At the tiny swat I chuckled. She wasn't nearly as vicious as she believed she was. "Laugh all you want but I don't need magick to kick your ass. Remember that." She sniffed slightly and I gave her legs a small squeeze, my thumbs stroking her skin, she kicked out with them. "Stop!" She sputtered slightly and I fought back a grin. I was wondering when she would tell me to stop.

"Stop what, pixie?" I turned my head, looking through the trees, trying my best to keep my voice as innocent as I could.

"You know what you are doing." There was a heavy dose of censure to her voice and I shrugged, giving my head a small shake. There was a faint pause as I continued walking before she let out a huff. *"Stop* touching my legs."

"Alright, pixie." I dropped her legs and she nearly immediately slipped down my back. She gave a small inhale and scrambled, trying to hold onto me. I once against grabbed her thighs, jostling her up higher on my back and she wrapped her arms around my neck, holding onto me tightly.

I could feel her heart thudding against me and she let out an aggravated sound. "Fucking *prick*!" She spat the words out and I grinned.

"You told me t' stop touchin' yer legs." At that I was cuffed upside the head once more. "So *violent* ye are." I actually liked that she was a little violent with me. It didn't hurt but I knew it must have made her feel better. It also showed that she was becoming more comfortable with me.

"I'll show you violent." She muttered the words out and I fought back a chuckle as I continued to walk through the Forest.

My instinct was at ease, it had settled last night. We had tended to the little female's feet, making sure they were cleaned and soothed by the herb concentrate we had made, and then we fed her. Despite how hungry we had been we let her eat a majority of the food, enjoying how excited she was with the small rabbit. Her little white teeth had eagerly tore cooked meat from bone and when she spotted us looking, her face would turn bright red and she would hide behind her hair.

I had no worries she would run off so I allowed her to wrap her chain around her ankle. I had urged her to speak, to tell me about her life but she had been very tight lipped, her face twisting up and her mouth pressing together tightly. She hadn't said a single word and so I told her about my life in the Northern Forests, told her about Lyxton and how we travelled with the herds of the deer. She had listened as if it fascinated her greatly but it hadn't been long before she started nodding off. After that it hadn't taken much coaxing for her to curl up in my arms once more.

It had been another night of torture as she clung to me, wrapping her leg around my hip as if coaxing me to indulge. I had spent the night recounting the various situations Lyxton and I had gotten into that had ended in serious pain. I knew it was better to recount the worst situations than to indulge myself in the little female before she was ready.

At the reminder I gently stroked her thighs once more as I adjusted her on my back once again. She stiffened, inhaling sharply but after a moment she let out a breath and relaxed. My mouth twitched upwards, she was getting used to me touching her. Not just that, her cheeks and neck would flush, she would start stammering, and her honeyed scent would sweeten with her desire.

"Do they always get that big?" The question was asked quietly and I fought back a smirk.

"Depends on what ye are referrin' t', pixie. Me or...?" I could already imagining her cheeks and neck flushing from my words and it amused me greatly.

She made a sound of disgust in her throat. "*Don't* be like that." Her voice pitched higher, letting me know I had struck not only a nerve but sparked something she was trying *very* hard to hide.

"Like what, pixie?" At that she made another irritated sound, hitting my chest with her fist. "I'm jus' *askin'*." I couldn't hide the smirk as I said it and she gave another highly irritated sound.

"The *trees*. Do they always grow that big?" She gave a jerky gesture to the pine trees around us and I looked up towards the tops of them. They were actually smaller than the ones up by my hunting grounds. The redwoods grew much bigger up there, nothing but large trunks as far as the eye could see. Some of them you couldn't even see the tops of.

"Sometimes bigger." I inhaled a deep lungful of air, the scent of clean water was growing stronger. I thought I had been imagining it at first but now I was sure there was a creek or a river close by. "These are evergreens, the redwoods near mine and Lyxton's huntin' camps are much bigger." I shifted my course and headed towards where the scent of water seemed the thickest.

"I don't believe you." There was an edge of suspicion to her voice before there was a pause as I shifted her up on my back, gently smoothing my fingers further up her thighs as I did so. Her thighs clenched around my sides slightly and that sweet scent of her desire deepened. She leaned back, removing her chest from my back and I fought back a smirk as she gave a small cough. "How much bigger?" She asked it lightly, giving another cough as her hands grasped my shoulders.

"Would need ten males t' go all the way 'round some." Lyxton and I generally hunted further up the mountains where the trees were less giant but that didn't stop the redwoods from growing that large.

"No way." She breathed it out and I gave a short nod. I turned my head to look at her and there was a look of distinct awe to her eyes as she leaned forwards. "What does it feel like walking among them?" Her gaze met mine and I stopped walking, frowning slightly. I never put much thought into how I felt about the world I lived in.

"I doona know, pixie." I met her gaze, her brown eyes were so expressive. "Like how ye felt when faced with the evergreens, more likely." I gave a slow nod as I said it and her cheeks flushed.

"Scared?" She looked away, resting her chin on my shoulder and I blinked slightly.

"The trees *scared* ye?" I was absolutely dumbfounded by that.

"Don't laugh!" Her face grew redder and she pinched her lips together. "I only ever read about them before and I never knew they would be so *big.*" She muttered the last few words out, giving a heaving sigh that showed her embarrassment with her admission.

I started walking once more. "Doona be embarrassed, pixie. If I had never seen anythin' tha' big I would have been more than startled as well." I could only imagine how it felt to not know of anything about the world around me and then be shoved right in the midst of it. Especially if I was as small as her.

"Really?" Her voice was small and I gave a small grunt of agreement.

"I wouldna lie t' ye, pixie." I tilted my head, I could hear the sound of crashing water and I headed in the direction that it was coming from and within a few moments I spotted a waterfall landing in a rather large and clear pool attached to a creek. "Look at tha'." I stepped out of the trees and slowly lowered Violet to the ground. "What ye think, pixie? Shall we have a swim?" She blinked up at me before looking toward the water.

I kicked off my boots and grabbed the bottom of my shirt, yanking it off and when I tossed it to the side Violet made a rather strange sound in her throat. I looked towards her and her eyes were wide and on my chest, her face slowly turning red.

I clenched my muscles, forcing them to show their definition for the little female. The flush moved down her neck and to her chest as she blinked, her pupils dilating. I smirked as her gaze moved across my chest, more than likely following my tattoos, the celtic patterns wrapped around my chest and my shoulders and I knew she had been interested in them previous from how her gaze lingered.

I moved closer to her and she seemed frozen, blinking at my chest before I reached out and lifted her chin with a knuckle. I stepped closer, nearly touching her as I looked down at her sweet face, her rosy lips parting as she breathed.

"I know ye like me, pixie. I can smell it." Such a sweet smell at that. I knew there was an issue with her being incompatible for offspring but I didn't care.

Her eyes widened and she swallowed. "No I don't." Her voice was slightly breathless and I could practically hear her heart beating rapidly in her chest.

"Ye can lie t' yerself, Violet, but you canna lie t' me." I reached down and grasped her thighs, lifting her up. Her scent was distracting and mouthwatering and she pushed against me even as her legs wrapped around my waist. I walked into the water, my hands tight on those pale and supple thighs.

"I don't." There was a note of fear to her voice, her gaze lingering on mine. I knew she wanted to fall towards me, wanted to give into her desire but there was a faint need to be pushed. I was more than willing to give her that final push.

Chapter Nine
Learn What Ye Fear

His hands were hot against me as he carried me further into the water, the cool water lapped at my feet, causing a strange mixture of soothing and stinging. My heart thudded hard in my chest, I was scared of what I felt. He made me ache and he had ignited a deep need within me but I knew wanting him would bring me nothing but death.

"I'm scared." I met his gaze and there was a great intensity within his blue eyes. I could see his desire, *feel* it, in that azure blue. It made my lower stomach tighten and desire rolled through me to match the desire I could see within him.

He slid a hand from my thigh to my lower back, holding me to him tightly as he lowered us both into the water. "Why, little pixie?" His voice was a low rumble and his fingers dug into my lower back muscles, rubbing the tension away and my eyes wanted to droop.

"They'll kill me if they find out." I swallowed at that. "I don't want to burn, Jax." I didn't want to learn what that felt like, I didn't want to feel the flames licking at my skin, feel them sear my nerves as they ate me alive.

His hand slid up my back to cup the back of my neck, forcing me to meet his gaze once again. "They willna put a hand on ye, Violet." His gaze was intense and it gleamed. I could feel the truth his words had as they rumbled over my skin. "I *swear* I will protect ye with everythin' tha' I am as long as ye are with me." His hand squeezed the back of my neck gently and I wanted to relax into him.

He had told me of his life before, told me of his twin, Lyxton, and their life they had. His voice had been calm and even as he told me about a life that had been so different from my own. His life had been within the Forests, with a family that had adored him, and he had wanted for nothing. He told me of how he and his brother had gotten into trouble growing up, how they had eventually gone their own way from the compound they had been raised.

His stories had brought me into a world I had never had the ability to experience and it had been the nicest thing anyone had ever done for me. I had been stuck in a world full of people taking from me, hurting me, leaving me in the dark about the world, that having someone give me a glimpse of something beyond the four walls that had always encased me was an indescribable feeling. I didn't know how to thank him for that. I didn't know what to say to get him to understand how much that meant to me.

My world was filled with pain and I knew I was lucky enough that I came out of it all half okay. Irma had made sure to let me know I was not loved or wanted but the witches I had grown up around, those in the prisons, had been my support. They came and went but they were the ones who brought me up, teaching me what it meant to be a witch, to be cared for, but I had never been actually loved. So hearing about Jax talking about his childhood or his brother, seeing his expression light up, and seeing what I had been denied my entire life, was something I couldn't put into words.

"Irma-" My voice caught in my throat and I closed my eyes tightly, bowing my head as I leaned forward, pressing my forehead to his shoulder as he stilled. Words caught in my throat, jumbling up until it created a lump. I gave a small cough before I ground my teeth together and pulled back, meeting his gaze once more. "Make her *hurt.*" Anger rolled through me at all I had been denied and taken from.

I had been taunted by her. Her holding my parents above me, telling me they hadn't wanted me, telling me they were happy with their other children, never giving me a second look as they left me to her. She broke my heart before I knew what it felt like to love and then she had crushed my spirit, infecting me with her poison.

"For what she has done." There was an angry burn to my eyes but I lifted my chin as I looked at him. I wanted to be strong in that, I didn't want to show weakness.

His eyes searched my face as one large hand slowly moved from my neck down my back, the heat of it a harsh and startling contrast to the cold of the water. "What has she done t' ye, pixie?" The question was asked in low tones that rumbled over my skin and I tightened my hands into fists.

"She gave me fear." My entire life I had lived steeped in it, never knowing who I was outside of it. Her brand of poison to keep me in line. I had never known a life without it and the glimpses I was getting where its shroud no longer covered me made me realize just how much I *hated* her for it.

"Do ye fear me, Violet?" His voice made me once again look at him, meet his gaze and I blinked slowly. I wanted to lie, to show I was brave but I couldn't.

"Yes." It came out on a wave of shame and I hated myself for it. He was a werewolf, yes. He was bigger than me, yes. But he hadn't hurt me, had protected me from a world that was dangerous and terrifying. He had sworn to never let anything hurt me while I was by his side. However it didn't stop the inherent fear I had with all things different and new.

He slid one of his hands around my side before grasping my fist, smoothing it out in his big palm. I shuddered at the feeling before he pressed my hand to his chest. His skin was hot against my palm and it sent a wave of heat through my nerves.

"Touch what scares ye, pixie. Learn so ye doona fear what is t' come." His voice was a low rumble and I shivered at the promise his words held. My mind whirled with images of what that would entail as I slowly moved my hand, shifting my legs so I was kneeling over his lap. I shifted my hand towards the dark patterns of his tattoos, letting my fingertips trace the patterns just as I had done in my dreams. I could feel my cheeks heating up despite the cool water that slowly swirled around my waist.

I brought my other hand up, sliding it across his chest to his other shoulder. I continued to trail my fingers over his tattoos. I was curious about the marks. I knew that werewolves healed quickly and that unless the wounds were deep.

"How did you manage to get these to stay?" I looked up at him and his mouth twitched upwards.

"Wolfsbane. Put it in the ink an' it stays under the skin." He tilted his head as he let me explore. He was a big male, it was obvious that there was some logistics about sex that would cause me a bit of am issue.

"Will you hurt me?" My voice came out slightly breathless as shifted on his lap, feeling his bulge pressed against the front of his pants. My cheeks heated even worse. There was *definitely* some logistical issues about what would fit where when it came to sex. I pushed the thoughts away as I slid my hands across the wide and hard muscles of his chest. His form made me want to sink my nails deep into his skin and hold him tight against me.

"I willna." His voice was a low rumble and he hands moved back to my hips, his strong fingers massaged me and I inhaled sharply as I shuddered underneath the contact. "Sweet females, dainty females, little pixies deserve t' be cherished an' pleased. Ye will be *well* pleased with me, Violet." At the words my breathing deepened slightly as my chest flushed. I ached for the werewolf I was currently touching and I swallowed hard.

"You really promise to protect me?" I met his gaze once more as my fingers trailed up his neck, following the beautiful patterns of his tattoos. I enjoyed the feeling of his skin underneath my hands and fingers and I loved the beautiful tattoos that encased his form.

His gaze burned into me and his chest rumbled with a silent growl. "While in my care, Violet, ye willna be harmed. I promise ye tha'." My name on his tongue made me shiver and lean towards him. I trailed my fingertips over his cheeks and I brushed my thumbs down his jaw, my breathing deepened further as I locked my gaze onto his lips.

"Will ye beg for it, Violet?" One of his hands moved up my back to grab the back of my neck, pulling me close enough that his breath brushed my mouth. "I willna touch ye till ye *beg* me." I didn't know how to respond to his words but his dominance made my lower stomach clench with sudden need.

I went to lean towards him and he pulled me away with a sinful grin before his hands slid down my sides to the hem of my dress. "Ye *will* beg me, Violet." He slowly lifted my wet dress. I shivered as the wet fabric moved over my heated skin as he pulled it off and tossed it towards the shore.

Slightly embarrassed, I crossed my arms over my chest and he gave a heavy rumble before he grabbed my wrists, pulling my arms away from my breasts. His hot gaze raked over my form and I inhaled deeply at the feeling it caused me.

"Doona hide from me, pixie." He removed his hair tie, letting the long strands loose before he leaned closer, trailing his nose up my neck, his hot breath brushing my ear. "I'm without words." I shuddered under the words, my mouth going dry.

His lips trailed the shell of my ear and goosebumps erupted over my skin. "*Stunnin'* ye are. Leave a male *achin'*." I flushed at the praise, feeling warm despite the coolness of the water that flowed around us. I grasped his arms with my hands, digging my fingers into his muscles as I lifted my chin, tilting my head to the side. "*Good pixie.*" The words were a rasping whisper as he buried his hand into my hair and pulled my head further to the side before his lips trailed over my neck, his stubble scratching my sensitive skin.

"What are you doing?" It came out like a gasp and he pulled away allowing my head to straighten as his azure gaze pierced into mine.

"Takin' care of ye." He shifted beneath me before standing up, holding me close. I shivered as the air moved over my wet skin. He slowly turned me around, his hands smoothing down my sides, leaving me shuddering underneath his hot touch. "Sit, pixie." He slowly pressed down on my shoulders and I slowly sat down in the water, listening to the sounds of water moving behind me. It didn't take long before his hands were on me once more. I arched my back, inhaling deeply at the feeling of his hands sliding over my skin.

He rubbed my skin, clearing away the dirt and sweat that had gathered over the past few days. I couldn't help the faint groan I let out as I leaned against his chest. He cleaned me, his broad palms washing away the remnants of the last few days.

After a few moments of relishing being clean, I inhaled sharply as he pulled me closer, his shaft felt overly large pressed against my ass and it throbbed against me. I blinked rapidly as he let out a low growl, the sound vibrating my back.

"Feel what ye do t' me, Violet. Ye could make me beg if I was a lesser male." He gave a low chuckle, the sound rolling over my skin in a way that felt indecent.

He slowly slid his hand up my stomach and his thumb brushed against the bottom of my breast. I bit my lip closing my eyes and just experiencing his touch. For a moment I could believe that there was more between us than just physical attraction.

Deep down there was a big part of me that wanted to be loved, to know how it felt to be loved by someone. It was easy to pretend that there was that aspect between us but I knew the truth. It was just sex.

His hand cupped my breast and I gave a small moan, arching my back to press my breast further into his palm. He pressed his face into the crook of my shoulder, his teeth dragging over my neck. His fingers moved over my nipple and I inhaled sharply.

Sure it was just sex but I knew it was going to be pretty fucking mind blowing. My body felt overly sensitive and each touch he gave me made me feel like liquid heat was rolling through my veins. No one had ever touched me the way he did. The fae males I had been with had been attentive but it had been a cool attentiveness, a passing thought to the situation.

His lips trailed up my neck and I shivered, wiggling with my need. My body felt over heated and when he shifted his hand to my other breast, his thumb stroking my aching nipple, I shuddered underneath the touch. I leaned firmer against him, pressing against his large and firm chest. My eyes fluttered closed and I leaned my head back against his shoulder as I gave into the feelings coursing through me.

His other hand slid down my stomach and I rolled my hips towards the touch, a needy sound escaping my throat. "Will ye beg me?" I nodded, unable to find words as my breaths came out in pants. "I need t' hear it, pixie." His words rolled over my skin and I let out a small whine as his teeth pinched my throat lightly.

"Please." I swallowed hard, turning my head as he let my neck go. "Jax, *please.*" I rolled my hips again and he chuckled, a rich sound that rolled over me and made my body feel slick and hot. He turned his head and captured my lips with his. I let out a moan against his mouth as I opened my lips, lapping my tongue against his. His hand cupped my sex suddenly and possessively and I inhaled deeply, letting out a groan at the heat of his hand against me.

He pulled away from the kiss. "Ye are like heated silk." He moved his fingers through my folds and the movements of his rough fingers against my sensitive skin made my mouth drop open as I moaned loudly. I shook, reaching up and digging my hand into his long hair, holding onto him tightly as he stroked my slick sex with talented fingers. He slipped one inside of me unexpectedly and I widened my knees, rolling my hips to get more. He gave a husky chuckle. "Like tha'?" I nodded quickly biting my lip as he slowly stroked my inner walls, pleasure making my body shudder and my vision nearly shake.

I arched my back, biting my lip harder to muffle the sounds that were wanting to escape. "Doona do tha', pixie. I want t' hear ye moan." His voice rolled over me as he pinched my jaw slightly, forcing me to stop biting down on my lip. "Ye want more?" He trailed his teeth over my neck once more and I gave a hasty nod. My worries about the logistics between us were quickly fading as he slid another finger into me, making me arch my back with a drawn out moan, my eyes fluttering shut.

"Ye like this, don't ye?" He murmured the words to me and I licked my lips as I nodded, barely able to think as he teased me mercilessly. My breathing became ragged and I couldn't focus on anything but the sensation of him stroking my sex and the heat it brought. "Do ye want me?" Everything tightened and I was barely able to nod as my muscles tightened in expectation of the peak I was going towards. He withdrew his fingers from me and I made a sound of protest. "Beg me, Violet." At the demand I inhaled sharply.

"Please, Jax." I needed that peak, needed to be burned by that fire.

"Turn around, pixie." He grasped my waist and helped me turned around, straddling his lap. He buried a hand in my hair and kissed me. It was dominating and claiming and I pressed closer to him, allowing his tongue to meet my own. I felt claimed and possessed by him and his touch as he lifted me up. I could feel him pressed against me and for a moment my worries about him being too big came back but they were chased away by his large hands grasping my ass firmly, giving a greedy grope before he slowly pulled me down onto him.

The feeling of being stretched around him bordered over the edge of pain and I leaned forward, biting his shoulder to muffle the slightly pained sound I made as I took him within me. My nails scratched against his skin and he grunted, his hands tightening on my ass as he shook slightly. A deep rumble vibrated his chest and I closed my eyes tightly, letting his shoulder go as I dug my nails into his skin, trying to transfer my pain to him.

"Easy, pixie. Relax." His voice was strained and I twisted my face up into a glower as I opened my eyes to look at him.

"Yah. Let me just do that." The sarcasm burned and I winced as I shifted over him. He gave a strained chuckle, his hands smoothing up from my ass and over my back before he leaned forward, pressing his lips to my collarbone. I felt overly full but I knew with a few moments I would be okay. He trailed his lips across my collarbone and towards the hollow of my throat. I blinked rapidly at the feeling it brought me, the heat moving through me rapidly.

He pulled back from my neck, looking at me as he reached up and stroked his thumb across my cheek. "Beautiful female." He breathed the words out and my cheeks flushed, his mouth twitched upwards into a smirk. "Still blushin' even when I'm buried deep inside ye." I could feel him throbbing within me and I made a face at him.

"Yah well, it's not like I get compliments all the time." Most guys liked to nut and run. It wasn't like they had to woo me all that much. I was perpetually lonely and sex was just one way I could pretend *someone* cared about me. It was pathetic, I knew that but it was who I was.

"But ye have sex." His intense expression didn't change as he cupped my cheek, lifting my chin.

"I do." I didn't want to be made to feel worse about my many partners. I already knew the reasons behind it was pathetic so I didn't want him to mock me for it.

"Yer males are pathetic if they wouldna tell ye of yer beauty." He drew me closer, brushing his lips across mine. "Female such as ye deserve t' be praised..." He kissed me more firmly and I relaxed towards him before he broke it, his lips trailing to my jaw line.

"Pampered..." His moved his hand as he brought his mouth to my neck, biting my skin and sucking, he released it with a faint sound of satisfaction.

"Cherished..." My skin tingled and I drew my nails across his skin and he slid his hands down my body to grasp my ass once more.

"*Pleasured.*" He drew me up his length and I gasp at the feeling it gave me before he pulled me down, thrusting up at the same time.

My mouth dropped open and a groan was wrenched from my throat. "Oh *goddess.*" I flexed my hands, shaking at the pleasure that ripped through me at the action.

"Ye like tha'?" His voice was smug but I didn't care as he once again drew me upwards. I dug my nails back into his skin and nodded quickly. I liked it *very* much. He leaned forward and bit my neck as he drew me down hard. A cry was wrenched from me as heat consumed me.

He continued his movements, drowning me in heavy pleasure. I gasped in air, leaning my head back to stare at the sky. I had never questioned the human ideals of heaven but I swore to their god the werewolf was taking me there.

My skin felt tight on my bones as I could feel the peak rising. Moans and gasps escaped my mouth in pants, drying out my lips. I was faintly aware of Jax muttering in my ear, his teeth trailing across my skin before he roughly took my lips with his, plunging his tongue into my mouth as if he were claiming it for his own. There was a dominant edge to him that made me shudder, made the pleasure burn that much hotter.

I dug my nails in deep, the world stretching out in my mind, time stopping for a few heartbeats until the orgasm crashed over me, a cry escaping my throat as I shook, nearly convulsing in Jax's grip.

"Fuckin' *beautiful.*" He growled the words into my ears as a deep growl rumbled in his chest. I felt like the world was wavering around me as he bit down hard on my shoulder, not breaking skin but leaving a mark. I writhed in his lap, biting my lip hard as tears came to my eyes. Everything was so intense and it seemed to be without end.

I met his eyes, my hands shaking and a moan was pulled deep from within me as it started to taper down. "Do ye want me?" I nodded before letting go of his shoulders and grabbing his face and kissing him, needing the contact as his thrusting got more rough and his grips grew harsher.

Within moments I could feel him coming and I gasped at the heat it brought me, pleasure seeping through my body as I leaned against his chest, resting my head on his shoulder as I wrapped my arms around him.

It was moments like this that made me crave sex. It was the closeness that I craved, the feeling of languid happiness that filled my veins. I craved it so much because I knew it was the only time in my small, small world I could ever feel cared for.

Chapter Ten
Chains and Bonds

Her form was perfect.

I smoothed my hand over her curves as she stood over me. I could feel the scars that lay on her skin, there were more than I had ever imagined but it didn't detract from the perfection that she was.

"*Beautiful.*" I wiped away the water from her skin and I watched as she flushed. I was intrigued by the fact that despite all I had done to her in the past two hours there were parts of her that still felt innocent. I was also realizing that I was grateful that despite her hard life that drew those scars on her skin that she was still sweet and innocent about the world. She didn't become jaded or hard to the world around her because of her suffering like she had all rights to do.

I pressed my lips to her navel, inhaling deeply. She smelled clean, pure, and feminine despite the bitter undertone that teased my nose. I gripped her hips and stroked her skin with my fingers. I didn't doubt that I would forever enjoy the feeling of soft skin underneath my fingertips.

"That tickles." She pushed me away slightly and I looked up at her as she made a face at me. I pressed my face to her stomach, rubbing my stubble against her skin until she giggled, struggling in my grip. I pulled her down to sit across my lap as the giggles continued to escape her.

I grinned as I grabbed my shirt from where I had hung it up over the small fire I had made. "Let's get ye dressed 'fore ye get cold." I helped her slip on my large shirt, enjoying how it swallowed up her form. I liked the thought she was naked beneath my clothing, that if I slid my hand underneath it I would be met with soft and supple flesh and nothing else. "Tha's right, *relax*." She leaned against my chest with a sigh as I trailed my fingers down her leg to where she had the long length of chain wrapped around her ankle. I slowly took it off, drying the tiny links with a piece of her torn dress that I had dried over the fire.

I knew nothing about why she had it on. I had been wondering if she simply didn't want to tell me or if she couldn't. She was a very tight lipped female, never truly saying anything about herself.

"Tell me somethin' about ye, Violet. Need t' know somethin'." I slowly wrapped the chain back around her ankle and she was silent for a moment before she shrugged.

"I don't know what to tell you. There isn't much that makes me, me." Her voice was quiet and nearly unsure. I felt for her to never truly be allowed to discover one's self because of confinement. My home compound had been stifling for me and Lyxton but to be stuck there with no escape, a chain around my ankle to hold me in place made me feel a flash of sadness for the female.

I finished with the chain and wrapped my arms around her, looking out over the water as the sunset reflected over the gently rippling surface. "Why do ye need the gold?" It was tucked away safely for her but I was curious as to why she had gone from fear to agitation when I had taken it.

"To buy my freedom from Irma." She said it evenly and calmly and that flare of guilt returned. She had been trying to escape Irma when I took her. I didn't regret my decision to take her, to regret it meant I would have missed burying myself into her silken heat repeatedly until we were both sated. I was not about to regret or miss that.

"Do ye think she will truly let ye go?" If I was such a witch, I wouldn't let her go no matter how much gold was offered to me. The thought of being given such a female to own and have made my cock twitch slightly.

She gave a small shrug, settling in my lap, shifting so her back rested against my chest. "It's about two thousand gold and all I can do is hope." She let out a wistful sigh as if her dreams of freedom were nothing but a fanciful dream.

"How did ye get tha' much?" For someone who was chained in the shop, I doubted she was paid so I was curious as to how she managed to get the gold. I doubted that she stolen it, she didn't seem the type of female to do that.

"Illegal potions. Sometimes sex." She said the last bit quietly, shame coating her words and it radiated off of her thickly. I was surprised by the admission. She didn't seem like the type of person who would be willing to do that. It made a rather dark feeling encase me.

"Ye sold yerself for a chance at yer freedom?" It didn't sit right with me that she was forced into a position in life that she would have to sell her sweet and heated body for a slim chance at freedom. Irma deserved nothing but utter torture for forcing a female to endure such a thing.

"You could say that, yes." She lowered head head, drawing up her knees to her chest. I slid my hands up her thighs and to her knees before sliding them down the inside of her thighs.

"I would give ye all the gold in the world if ye continue t' let me between yer silky thighs." I would pamper her endlessly, cherish every inch of her flesh, and shower her in gold coins just for the privilege to be with her but never for the slim chance at her buying freedom.

"It’s not funny." There was an edge to her voice as she grabbed my wrists, stalling my movements.

"I'm not laughin', pixie." I nuzzled her neck, nipping a her skin. She shuddered against me, making a muffled noise in her throat.

"What do you mean?" Her voice was slightly strained and I grinned before brushing my lips down her throat.

"Do ye think tha' I didna enjoy ye? Ye're pure *perfection* an' ye think I wouldna wish t' spend all the gold I could t' keep between yer thighs?" I moved my hands lower, ignoring her weak grip on my wrists. "Silly female." I nipped at her ear. "Do ye wish for me t' stop teasin' ye here?" I slowly cupped her pussy and she cut off a slight moan as her knees spread slightly, giving me more room.

"Tell me, Violet." I gave a low growl and she leaned her head back against my shoulder.

"I don't." She breathed the words out and I drew my teeth down her neck.

"Ye doona what?" I spoke against her skin and she shivered heavily.

"I don't want you to stop." She gasped it out as I stroked her slickening flesh with my fingers.

"*Never* think I am jokin with ye when it comes t' bein between ye're thighs and slidin' deep within ye." I wrapped my other arms around her waist sliding my hand between the buttons to grasp at her heated side. "Do ye want me t' pleasure ye again?" I slowly slid my fingers up towards her breast and she nodded. "Let me hear ye say it, pixie." I liked hearing her tell me that she wanted me, liked hearing that breathy and needy tone of her voice.

"Yes, Jax." She nodded turning her head to look up at me, her lips parting in an invitation.

"Aye what, Violet?" I narrowed my eyes as I stroked the bottom swell of her breast, teasing her skin as she wiggled between my legs. My cock swelled in response to the sweet and wet heat that was slowly soaking my fingers from her pussy.

"I want you to pleasure me." Her brown eyes pleaded with me and I grinned, hunger rising up within me thick and heavy.

"*Gladly.*" I captured her lips with my own, demanding her submission and her compliance with my demands. I would pleasure and please her but only with her complete and total submission underneath me and she would enjoy *every single second* of it.

Chapter Eleven
Flowers and Fairytales

I fiddled with the ends of Jax's shirt as I stared at the ground, looking for the herbs that Jax had described. I was growing a bit agitated because everything looked the same to me.

"Like this, pixie." He came closer, holding out several plants for me to look at. He took a thinner one with broad leaves and light purple flowers. "Holy basil, helps with stress and headaches, s'pecially if ye make it int' a tea." I took it from him, looking it over, trying hard to memorize what it looked like before he showed me another one. It was very stalky with thin leaves and bright yellow flowers. "St. John's Wart, ye know its for bruises and swellin'. I used it on ye're feet." He held it out to me and I nodded.

I gently touched the petals of the flower, my feet did feel worlds better than they had. He held out a strange looking plant with four thin, purple striped petals.

"'S andrographis. Helps with colds and chest coughs." I had to try very hard to keep my eyes on the plants he was handing me and not on his chest or stomach. As I was wearing his shirt, he was uncovered and fully exposed to my gaze. His muscles moved easily underneath his skin and showed his awe inspiring strength.

He handed me another flower, this one was yellow and orange with many different little petals. I took it with a smile, it was bright and cheery. "Calendula, helps with rashes and healin'." He took it from me and snapped off most of its stem before tucking the flower into my hair. "Also good for makin' females look pretty'." He said it casually and my face heated up immediately, his chuckle soon following.

I lifted the plants up closer to my face to distract myself from the growing heat in my cheeks. "How do you keep them straight?" He had been rattling off the names and pointing the herbs out so quickly it made my head spin.

"I've had years of it, pixie. Doona worry, ye'll get it eventually." He looked out into the trees before his large hand slid across my back and grasped my side. He tugged me close before scanning the area.

"Do you see anything?" I pressed closer to him, looking around warily.

"No, jus' watchin'." His strong fingers stroked my side and I shivered underneath the touch. It was rather amazing, I had never had a male simply touch me and make me clench with need immediately. I knew it had a lot to do with how well he managed to satisfy me completely and totally. He had left me limp with bliss and shuddering with after shocks of intense pleasure.

"Where are we going?" I looked up at him and he gave a small shrug.

"Doono, pixie, tryin' t' figure out where tha' bitch would be." There was a heavy edge of hate to his voice, his fingers tightening on me before he roughly pulled me to his chest. I gave a small sound of surprise before he crushed his lips to mine. I grasped his shoulders, swaying towards him as a hand slid down my back to grab my ass. I gasped against his mouth and he slipped his tongue inside to tease my own.

He pulled back suddenly, a growl vibrating his chest as he reached down further and slipped his hand underneath the shirt, his hot palm sliding across the bare skin of my ass.

"I'm gunna kill her, torment her for ye." He reached down with his other hand, grasping my other ass cheek before lifting me up.

I wrapped my legs around his waist as he walked forwards and my back met the rough bark of the tree. His words made my lower stomach and sex clench with need.

"You will?" I met his gaze, wanting his honesty, his hot hands on me bringing me pleasure when I knew those hands would destroy the Elder witch who had hurt me so much.

"Aye, pixie, gunna torment her slow." He slowly ground himself into my bare sex, the rough fabric of his pants rubbing against my sensitive skin, sending a shocking jolt of pleasure through me. "Draw her death from her for ye." He tightened his hands on my ass, leaning towards me as he brushed his lips against mine.

"Make her pay for what she has done t' ye." He gave me a rather gentle kiss that had me whimpering, wrapping my arms around his neck. I closed my eyes, pressing closer to him before he yanked back from me, removing one hand from my ass before he expertly undid the top three buttons of the shirt, baring my heaving chest to his view.

I arched my back underneath it, it felt like a physical touch. I bit my lip tightly. "What have I said, Violet. I want t' hear ye." At the demand I immediately let my lip go. "Do ye want me?" At the question I nodded quickly, his gaze darkened as he gave me a searing kiss that had a deep moan escape me as he pulled away. "Do ye want me t' kill the witch?" I was nearly breathless as I nodded.

"Want me t' hurt her?" He slowly ground into me again, making my eyes flutter close and my nails dig into the skin of his shoulders.

"*Yes.*" I hissed the word out and he palmed one of my breasts, my nipple tightened against his rough palm.

"How?" His accent was thick and I scratched my nails against his skin at the question as I tried to think through the pleasure his rocking hips were giving me. I was trying very hard to fight against the slick heat that was enveloping me.

"Show her how brutal werewolves can be." I gasped the words out, meeting his gaze. I wanted Irma to feel that pain. I wanted her to suffer what I did when she told Florence where I was, where she told her about the time check spell on the chain.

"Aye, I can do tha', pixie." His eyes gleamed with pleasure and desire and that ferality that let me know his teeth would be planted somewhere on my body, making marks but not breaking skin. "Will tear her apart. Ye like tha'?" I nodded quickly as the heat shuddered through me. I liked the thought of her finally being paid back for all she had done to me and the other witches that had been detained in Coven Thirteen.

"I like tha', Violet, ye're my vicious little pixie, aren't ye?" He grinned at me, showing me those sharp teeth. He lowered his head, his hot breath washing over my lips, making me ache for a kiss. "Do ye want me t' please ye?" At that I gave an eager nod. I felt overheated and aching, my vision darkening with my need for release.

"Do ye want me t' slide deep int' ye?" He brushed his lips across mine and I gave a small whimper, trying to kiss but he pulled back. "Ye have t' beg me." It was a sharp order and I leaned towards him, my eyes fluttering as his fingers brushed my sex from his grip on my ass.

"*Please*, Jax." I needed him. I needed him to slid his shaft deep into my sex to make that intense peak shatter around me once more.

"What do ye need?" The words were a hot whisper in my ear before his teeth trailed over the shell of my ear. I shivered, gripping his shoulders tightly.

"You inside me." My cheeks flushed hotly as I said it. I had never been so verbal having sex before and it sent a small thrill through me.

"Aye, an' I wish t' be inside ye sweet little pussy." He shifted his hand before he kissed me, claiming my mouth once more.

My head spun as pleasure washed over me at his kiss, his lips moving expertly on mine as his knuckles brushed my slick sex as he undid his pants and I rolled my hips towards him, needing that contact. He withdrew his hands and his hot shaft pressed against my folds and I let out a groan at my sudden need to be filled.

"Please, Jax." I rolled my hips, grinding against his shaft, needing to feel it within me. He had made me crave his touch and his member throbbing deep within me. I *ached* for it.

"Ye want it?" He thrust his member against my sex, teasing me with what I so wanted.

"*Yes*!" I felt so overwhelmed by everything that was happening and the sensations that he was causing with in me. I felt almost frantic with my desire and need for him. He didn't seem inclined to sate me as he continued his slow thrusts against my sex.

I felt tormented and unbearably hot and achy as I writhed in his grip, tightening my legs around his waist as I whimpered. I fought to find my voice, needing the torment to stop.

"Don't you want me?" I rolled my hips against his thick shaft as frustrated tears sprung to my eyes. I needed for him to be inside me, to sate the burning ache I felt.

"Aye, pixie. I do." His voice was strained before he captured my lips with his, shifting his hips. I could feel him pressed against me before he fed his length into my aching sex. I shuddered at the feeling, it was slightly uncomfortable to be stretched around him but it wasn't as painful as the first entrance he made into me. In fact it was *much* more pleasurable and heated, making me moan into his mouth as he twined his tongue around my own. I gripped him tightly as he pulled away from me.

"Ye're so tight and hot." He nipped at my ear before trailing his teeth over my neck, soothing the slight mark with his tongue.

I couldn't respond to him as he started thrusting into me. Each sharp movement of his hips made me gasp as I drug my nails across his skin, marking him as he was marking me.

"Ye're fuckin' *exquisite.*" He growled the words into my ear and I gave a heavy moan, my slick sex pulsating around him, a warning of my impending orgasm. "Tha's it, come for me, pixie." His thrusts grew harder and rougher and a keening cry escaped my throat as the peak grew hotter and more intense around me.

"Come on me, Violet, show me ye like my cock." At his crude words I tensed and the peak shattered around me and my mind swirled around with pleasure as the world seemed to disappear from around me. All that I could perceive was the thick and hot pleasure of his length thrusting into me and his hot hands and mouth travelling over my sensitive skin.

I met his movements, my hips moving in sync with his, my body demanding more pleasure even as I shook from it. Colours flashed behind my eyelids as Jax took my mouth in a dominating kiss once more. His movements grew harsher, his hands gripping me to the point of pain, and his thrusts became more erratic before he pulled back from the kiss and bit my throat. I inhaled deeply as another peak hit me unexpectedly, I bathed him in my release as he came within me, the heat making me roll my hips uncontrollably.

My breathing came out in pants and my heart thudded hard in my chest as I came back to myself, the lingering pleasure still making me tremble. I leaned my head against the tree I was pressed against and Jax let my throat go, brushing his lips against the sore skin as a deep and possessive growl rumbled out of him. A large hand sunk into my hair and he pressed his forehead to mine.

"Ye are blessed by the moon, Violet, ye can make a male weak." His words were rasping against my skin and I felt my cheeks flush slightly before he kissed me again, making my eyes flutter close with a faint feeling of bliss.

It felt stupid but a part of me felt like he was the male I would kiss for the rest of my life and I knew thinking like that would only get me hurt.

Chapter Twelve
Distractions

I carried the little witch through the forest, she hummed lightly, her chin resting on my shoulder. I was content with the little female, despite the very slight bitter undertone to her scent. For me, it didn't matter. I had a willing female that seemed to crave my attentions. It also settled me to take care of a female, to provide for one. It made it very clear to me that once I got my brother back that I would need to find myself a female to carry on my line with.

As much as I liked the witch, she wasn't compatible with me for offspring and I wanted babes. I wanted a female who would grow round with my child. I wanted to be there as she created life within herself, to watch the changes in her body. There was a small part of me that wondered how the little pixie would look if my seed took within her but it was easy to push it away with her scent. The bitterness was all it took for the thoughts to stop.

"What are you going to do when you find your brother?" Her question was light as she shifted her arms around my neck.

"Go home." Take him and go back to our hunting grounds before going to the compounds to find suitable females for both of us.

"Oh." It was a small sound and I switched directions, I could faintly scent humans and I knew that we would be coming towards a human settlement.

"What will ye do with the witch dead?" I wondered about the little witch, what she would do with her freedom. I could only imagine that she would like to return to a Coven to be with other witches or perhaps find herself with a warlock.

The thought made me wish to bare my teeth. I didn't particularly like the thought of another male stroking her skin, feeding themselves into her heated and sweet pussy. I didn't want to think about any other males that would be with her because it gave me an urge to destroy the males who thought they could touch her as I did.

She didn't answer me and I jostled her slightly. "Pixie, what will ye do with the witch dead?"

There was a pause before she made a small sound. "I don't know." Her voice was tiny and I frowned.

"How is it ye don't know?" She should have had a plan. If I had been stuck for years I would have had a plan for my freedom.

"I've never known anything but Irma and her world. I don't know what I would do outside of it." She had a good point but she sounded perturbed and her voice trembled as if she were scared of the uncertainty her future held. "I don't know." It was once again that tiny and uncertain voice that made me frown. It made that small part of me wish to take her away and pamper her as she should have been.

"Well ye will have yer gold. With it ye can buy a good life for yerself." With me killing the Elder witch it would leave her with the significant amount of gold. She could get herself a small place and start a new life. It made me feel better to know that she would have the ability to take care of herself.

"I could go to my parents." She said it carefully at first before a bit of hopefulness entered her tone at the end.

"Aye." I gave a slow nod at that, she would be well taken care of with her parents.

She made a small sound in her throat. "Do you think they would want to see me?" There was a timid tone to her voice, as if she were hesitant to believe her parents would want her back.

"*Aye*, ye're their babe. They will wish t' be reunited with ye." I couldn't imagine what situation where they *wouldn't* wish to see her. If I was separated from my child there would be nothing in the universe that would stop me from finding them once more.

"Irma always told me they gave me to her and never wanted me." The way she said it made me bare my teeth and tighten my grip on her legs.

"She's a cruel bitch, pixie. Doona put any faith int' her words." I couldn't imagine why she would ever believe anything that female said to her. She should never lose faith in the parent's love for her because I was certain they loved her dearly.

She was silent for a few moments before she nodded. "You're probably right." She wiggled on my back before tapping my collar bone. "Set me down so

I can look for herbs." At her words I immediately let her down, watching her as she tugged down my shirt around her smooth thighs as she tucked her hair behind her ears before she smiled at me.

"Find some St John's Wort an' bring it back t' me." I crossed my arms over my chest and leaned against a nearby tree. I nearly smirked at the blush that crossed her face as she stared at my chest.

She was a lusty female, no matter how hard she tried to hide it. It took her a second before she nodded and headed away from me. I watched her carefully, making sure she didn't wander too far from me. I could still smell the human town that was not far from us. I wasn't sure of the exact distance but it was no greater than two miles.

I watched as the little female crouched down, looking at different plants on the forest floor. I was pleased that the female was so interested in the healing herbs. It showed an inclination towards the healing arts. There weren't enough people who showed such an inclinations and healers weren't common. There was only one or two shared between several compounds and it caused many issues. Werewolves didn't get sick or hurt frequently but battles happened often and serious wounds needed to be tended to.

Time passed by as the little pixie flitted to me and back, showing me different herbs and flowers and trying to find the ones I told her to look for. However the more I stood there watching her, the more I felt uncomfortable and agitated. It took a several minutes of this uncomfortable feeling within me before my instinct started to creep back to life. It went around my rib cage and moved through my veins. It made my muscles twitch and my bones ache.

Find brother

The words were hissed at me and I stiffened underneath them as the uncomfortable feeling I had been experiencing was shown. I narrowed my eyes as I looked at the little witch. I had been too distracted by her to remember to look for my brother. My instinct had been satisfied with the female but now it was going back to our prime objective, finding Lyxton.

I looked towards where the scent of humans were coming from. I needed to find more clues as to where the Elder witch was so I could find my brother. I glanced at the little female as she slowly picked some herbs further from me. I narrowed my eyes further as I turned to look back in the direction of where the town was.

"Pixie." My voice came out a bit more gruff and she jumped but immediately headed right for me. Once she drew close enough I crouched down, gesturing to her foot. She held it up for me and I unwrapped the chain from around her ankle.

When I glanced up at her she gave me a puzzled look as I held the thin chain in my hand "What are you doing?" I looked at her, judging my chances. If I brought her to the town there was a higher chance of me being ambushed by a group of witches and losing the little female all together. I could leave her in the forest and she would be safe and there would be no chance of witches coming after me aggressively because of her but I didn't want her to wander off and get lost.

"Jax?" Her voice wavered slightly but I ignored her as I looked up at the tree and let my claws come out. I jumped high up on the trunk, digging my claws into the tree before I threw the chain over a high branch, tying it tightly. "What are you doing?" Her voice rose in pitch and I dropped down to the forest floor.

"Goin' t' the town." I looked down at her and her brown eyes widened.

"Take me with you." Her voice came out in a rush as she looked up at the branch where I had put the chain.

"I canna do tha', pixie." I shook my head. "Witches would come after me, could hurt ye in the process. Canna allow tha'." I looked towards the direction of the town. "I'll be back, doona worry 'bout it." I started to walk away and she grabbed my arm, I could hear her heart thudding in her chest with her fear.

"Don't!" It was a fear filled word and I shook her grip off before turning and grasping her face.

"It will be fine, pixie, doona worry. I'll be right back." I kissed her hard before I let her go and moved away. There was no reason for her to worry. I would be back and everything would be fine.

Chapter Thirteen
Broken Promises

My heart pounded in my chest as I watched him walk away. "Don't leave me out here, Jax!" I shouted the words at him, my tone almost hysterical. He didn't respond as he walked further away. I felt panic rising up in my chest and it rose high enough to touch the back of my throat. I whirled around and grabbed the chain he had tied around a branch above my head. I yanked hard on the chain but it held fast. The knot was too high up for me to reach and I looked over my shoulder. "Jax!" I didn't want to be left alone out in the Forest.

I spotted a fallen branch and I ran for it but the chain immediately went taut. I fell just a few feet from the branch. My breathing started to increase and I tried hard to reach the branch but no matter how hard I reached for it, it remained just out of reach of my fingers.

I turned, sitting down and yanked on the chain around my ankle. I cursed the fact it wouldn't shift off my ankle. I had tried it thousands of times over the years but I never felt the incredible need to escape as I did now.

I grabbed the chain tightly in my hands, pulling hard on it. The tree branch it was tied it didn't even move and I inhaled, my chin trembling. The feeling of being trapped was growing worse and I jumped to my feet, going back to the tree, grabbing the chain and trying to climb up the side of the tree. I kept slipping, my hands rubbing raw on the chain and my knees and feet being scraped up by the bark.

I slowly climbed, doing my best to stay up and when I reached for the branch, seeing it just over my head but I fell. I hit the ground hard and tears blurred my eyes, I had been *so* close to grabbing the branch. I let out an aggravated sound, yanking on the chain, ignoring the pain of my cut palms. I glowered up at the branch, my heart pounding rapidly in my chest and I looked around warily.

Something seemed to be hanging in the air, an edge of expectation that made a shiver run down my spine. I shoved my hand into my hair as I bit my lip hard. I wanted to get out, I needed to leave. Jax had been gone for nearly twenty minutes and the longer he was gone, the less I felt safe. *Something* was coming, I didn't know what it was but I knew it wasn't good.

I moved around one side of the tree, trying to see how far I could go and also grabbing the chain and rubbing it against the tree, hoping to weaken it. I knew it was a fool's hope, I had seen the spells Irma had placed on it and I knew the chain was indestructible as long as she was alive. Time crawled on as I tried each and every way that I could to try and free the chain from the branch but it all proved fruitless.

My heart pounding harshly in my chest and I wiped my sweaty, stinging palms on Jax's shirt, my mouth dry. I was one hundred percent trapped and it made the panic in me grow that much more. I shook my head, leaning against the tree, sobs fighting their way up in my chest. I looked around, feeling like I was being watched and my hands shook violently. The fear soured my stomach and bile touched my throat.

"Witch." At the growled voice, the hair rose up on the back of my neck and I slowly turned my head. A werewolf with gleaming eyes stalked towards me and I pressed myself against the tree.

I blinked at him warily and shook my head. "I'm not alone." My heart hammered hard in my chest as he grinned, his teeth sharp in his mouth. I knew how those felt tearing into flesh and my breathing increased until my breaths came out in panicked pants.

"Lie." The word was garbled. "I watched." I scrambled away from him, tripping over my chain as I did so. My breathing increased to the point where I was nearly gasping as he loomed over me.

My chain yanked tight, letting me know there was no where I could go and I held up my hand. "Stop!" I shouted it out and he paused, my heart in my throat. "I haven't done anything to you!" I didn't know who this male was, I had no clue why he was coming towards me. No clue why he looked so *angry*.

His eyes flashed yellow and he seemed to be growing larger, puffing himself up. "Betrayed Bam. Betrayed Bo." At that my heart seemed to stop in my chest. It was the werewolf that had been with Miranda.

Fear made my vision swim and my face pale. "I didn't!" I wanted to tell him why I told, wanted to save myself but my throat closed, the spell refusing me the words that would save me. He moved closer, stepping down on the chain while I tried to scramble backwards and away. "*Please!*" He grabbed my ankle and his claws sunk in as he yanked me towards him.

"I didn't mean too! The chai-" My throat tightened and I would have been sent into a coughing fit but claws raked through my throat, my coughs garbling as the heat of my blood spilled over my skin.

I stared up at the male, watching his face turn angular as fur pushed through his pores. I gasped for air, gasped for the life that was seeping through my fingers as I clutched at my throat. My vision seemed to flicker, one minute he was human and the next he was a beast.

I couldn't even scream as his teeth sunk into my belly, ripping through flesh and tearing through muscle. Pain exploded in my skull, my vision went white and when it returned I could see the werewolf tugging on something deep inside me, could feel it but the pain was growing less.

I couldn't breathe, my throat was no longer capable of inhaling air and my lungs no longer capable of holding it as he dug clawed hands up into my rib cage. I looked away, looking at the dark canopy of the evergreen tree I lay underneath. I felt light yet heavy, a familiar feeling of death that coated the pain. I was just thankful he had taken my throat before he started on my stomach because I couldn't feel it anymore. I was thankfully fading, going further and further away. My vision growing darker and my body growing colder as I bled.

It was a relief to no longer feel the searing pain, a relief to be without how badly it hurt but curiously my chest burned and ached like a thousand brilliant suns as an echo of accented words rolled over me. My eyes burned and when I blinked, my eyes closing at the heaviness that descended over me, the tears seared my skin like fire.

He promised I wouldn't be hurt.

He *promised.*

Chapter Fourteen
Twisted Aftermath

Havenbrook had nothing I had needed but I had managed to steal some clothes for the little pixie. As much as I enjoyed her wrapped up in my shirt I knew that it wasn't practical for her to be running around without proper clothes. The air was turning and fall would be closing in on us. If she was going to be out in the Forest she would need to be properly clothed.

I had expected the human settlement to provide me with *some* information about the Covens around but no one had been willing to speak to me. That and no one had seemed to understand my question at all.

I had a sneaking suspicion the Witch covens spelled the town to forget about them, which made sense especially considering who I was hunting. My lip curled up at the reminder of the cruel bitch. I did not know what she had done to the little pixie but it was not good and I would repay her cruelty tenfold.

I shifted my direction towards where I had left Violet and I paused, my hair standing up on the back of my neck. I tilted my head, listening for something, anything, but there was nothing but a still silence, not even the small animals were making sounds. I narrowed my eyes and moved towards the area slowly.

"Pixie?" I called it out trying to listen for the predator that had quietened the animals but there was nothing. That thick silence was all that answered me. I knew that silence, it followed in my wake.

I inhaled deeply, trying to scent out what predator was close by when I froze. The scent of blood coated the back of my throat thickly. I snarled bolting towards the tree, crashing through the brush. I skidded to a stop, blood splashed the area, it gathered in pools on the ground and I narrowed my eyes.

Rage rose up thick in me as I looked at the bloody scene. Vibrant red was everywhere. I stalked forwards, dreading what I would find. I couldn't scent anything out, the blood was so thick. I had a hot feeling in my gut, the feeling of a heavy guilt that I had left her out here to be harmed.

I looked around, not just harmed, I had a feeling that someone had died and the little female was the likely victim. No magick, small, and chained to a fucking tree. I moved further into the area and I looked around again, there was no sign of anything around. All I could see was blood, it splattered everything. I turned my head, taking another step and a pale, delicate foot caught my attention.

"Violet!" I made my way towards her quickly. She was curled up, leaning against the tree, blood streaking her skin as she trembled. I grasped her quickly, looking her over, searching for the wounds I knew she must have had. Her skin was pale, nearly grey, and almost icy cold. If it wasn't for the movement of her chest and the beating of her heart, she looked like a corpse.

"Pixie, talk t' me." I jostled her, moving my hands over her skin as I searched for the wounds that I could not see.

She said nothing but slowly turned her head to look at me. There was a hollowness to her gaze that was eerie and made shivers down my spine. She opened her mouth as if going to speak but then closed it without a word.

"What happened, pixie?" I asked it softly. Her skin was sticky with blood and there was blood everywhere but she had no marks I could see or feel.

Her form shook and she stared out into the Forest. "I.... I'm fine." Her voice was a rasping whisper as if her throat was raw and sore. "I'm fine." She gave a slow nod, closing her eyes.

I gave her a small shake, baring my teeth. "I didna ask tha', Violet. What *happened?*" I needed to know what had happened. I needed her to explain to me why there was blood everywhere and she was unmarked. I gave her another small shake and she slowly shrugged but said nothing. "Ye *need* t' tell me." She didn't even move at my order.

It took a few moments after I squeezed her shoulder for her to react. "Where were you?" She looked at me, that empty look still in her eyes.

"The town, pixie, I told ye." She looked too pale, she was too cold. I gathered her close but she didn't seem to be even aware I was holding her.

"Where *were* you?" She repeated the question and I pressed my face to her hair, my eyes narrowing. I could smell the blood on her, it was thick in her hair and smeared across her body.

The entire situation was strange, someone should have been dead with the amount of blood that was around the area but the little pixie was alive, a bit off but alive.

"Havenbrook, Violet. Tha's where I was." I stroked her hair and my hair came back red with blood. I stared at the sticky liquid that coated my palms and my instinct hissed its anger and confusion.

"Havenbrook?" Her voice showed a bit more life as she moved in my arms, looking up at me.

I nodded at her, squeezing her tightly. "Aye, pixie. Havenbrook." I looked around carefully, wondering if anyone was hanging around. I couldn't smell anyone but the blood was so thick that it covered up any scents there could be. "What happened?" I *needed* to know what happened but once again she went completely silent.

I let her go and climbed up the tree, untying the chain from the branch. I landed beside her but she didn't even flinch. I reached down, helping her to her feet but she didn't seem to even respond to that, just blinked while looking at nothing. "Pixie, are ye okay?" There was another extremely long pause before she moved.

"I'm fine, Jax." Her tone was empty and hollow before she looked up at me. "I'm dirty." It was a blunt set of words and I looked at her before nodding.

"Aye, ye are." I grasped her hand gently, she felt so delicate underneath my fingertips. "Let's get ye clean." I lead her carefully through the trees, away from the bloody scene. I would take her back to the small creek that we had followed. I would clean her and she would be better after that. I glanced at her pale form streaked with red. Everything would be okay once she was cleaned and taken care of.

"Havenbrook." She muttered the word out and I squeezed her hand gently, looking around.

"Aye, pixie. Havenbrook." A tiny town that had done nothing for my search and had me returning to what looked to be a murder scene.

"Havenbrook." She muttered the word again and I looked at her carefully.

The more I looked at her, the less okay she seemed. "Are ye okay? Ye doona look fine, pixie." She looked less that okay and it bothered me.

"I'm fine." It seemed like an almost robotic rely to me, something she said because she wanted to keep me quiet.

"Ye aren't, Violet." I shook my head quickly, pulling her close as I lifted her chin.

She stared up at me, no expression to her face as she gave a slow blink. "I'm alive, Jax. I'm fine." Her voice was even and didn't waver a single inch. Her wording confused me slightly. "I'm dirty. I need to be cleaned." She looked up at me and I gave another nod at that.

"Aye, pixie." As much as I didn't want to simply accept that explanation, I knew she wasn't going to say much more. I just hoped that once she was clean she would be a bit more forthcoming with information.

My instinct was just as confused with her actions and what happened to her when I had been gone. It hissed at me with words I couldn't understand but it was angry and it was telling me to do something but I didn't know what. It wanted me to protect her but I didn't know from what.

The little female was some how in trouble but for the first time in my life, I didn't know how to fix it.

Chapter Fifteen
Paid in Full

I stared up at the dark sky. I could see a few bright stars through the evergreen boughs and despite the cover the Forest brought, the moon full and its light permeated the area. It cast everything in an eerie glow, made the world seem surreal and haunting. It matched how I felt. Nothing felt right since the time check had brought me back.

I shivered slightly. I was so *cold.* Dying so violently always seemed to seep the warmth from the very core of my being. I was cold right through to my bones and no matter how warm Jax was, that heat did not sink into me. I could never forget that feeling, the feeling of ice overtaking the center of my being and refusing to let go. I took me a *very* long time to warm up after it happened, sometimes I feared I would never warm up again.

Jax's arm rested over my waist, his breath brushing over my neck. He hadn't been far from my side since he had returned from Havenbrook and found me. My chest *ached* at that. He had promised me I would be okay, that he would keep me safe but he had left me in the Forest, tied me to a fucking tree, and *left* me. Tears sprung to my eyes at the thought. There was something fucking wrong with me. Horrible things always happened to me and I didn't know why.

I turned my head to look at Jax and pain lanced my chest at the sight of his relaxed face. I wanted to cry. Everything in my life was fucked up. I just couldn't deal with it anymore, couldn't play pretend with him anymore. I slowly slipped out from underneath his arm and got to my feet.

My stomach ached from the remnants of the death I had endured and I slowly started walking west. That was the direction Jax told me the town was in. I winced at that. I was *so* tired of people hurting me, of them breaking promises, or using me.

I trudged through the woods, keeping my eyes on the northern star, making sure I was continuing in the right direction. The night was dark but I could see by the light of the moon. I tried my best to walk quietly, trying not to alert Jax to my movements. He was asleep but I didn't trust that he wouldn't wake up and stop me from leaving.

I felt unsafe as I walked further into the forest but I pushed through it. I wasn't safe no matter where I was. I just had to continue on and push through it until I found a place I could hide from the world. Being taken from the shop had taught me a cruel lesson. The world was beautiful and magnificent but the more it appeared the way the more it would hurt you. It would tear you apart and break your heart. I hated my life in the shop but it was better than what I felt now.

Jax had lied to me. He had told me some pretty words and I had stupidly fell for them. I had foolish hopes that we could be together. That me being with him, taking that risk, meant he would do the same for me. I had thought that he would protect me and care for me and that he would *want* me.

I was wrong. He had spun a pretty web of lies to make me comfortable so he could get his jollies off.

None of what he said was true. *None* of it. He was going to leave when he found his brother, was going to walk away and never look back. It fucking *hurt* because he had shown me this amazing and new world but would have left me in it without a guide. Just leave with a simple thank you for the sex and never think about me again.

Tears seared my eyes and rolled down my cheeks as I shivered, wrapping my arms around myself. The tears felt overly hot against my cold skin. It was always so cold. I couldn't get warm. I rubbed at my arms as I looked around. I could see a clearing ahead but I wasn't sure what it was. I looked up at the sky, picking out the northern star and reassuring myself that I was walking to the right way before I made it to the clearing.

I paused, a black top road lay in front of me and when I looked down it I could see a large sign with Havenbrook written on it with a one beside it. I slowly crept forward, making my way to the road and then walking towards the sign. I was certain that the road would lead me to where I needed to go. I wanted to see my parents, to have someone look at me and tell me it would be okay, that they would be there for me.

I sniffled, wiping at my nose. I didn't have to worry that Jax would wake up and follow me anymore. I had been walking for a long while and I knew any sounds I would make now, he had no chance of hearing. I coughed, rubbing at my arms again, trying to get rid of the ice in my veins that wouldn't go away.

I walked and pondered what my parents would be like, what type of life they lived and how much they must had missed me. I wondered if they missed me as much as I missed them. I hadn't been given the chance to meet them and I missed them with everything that I was. I had held onto the hope that they would one day come for me, that they would take me from Irma. Now I just wanted to ask them why they had left me with her for so long.

That thought tugged at something inside my chest and my stomach rolled violently at the memory of the werewolf doing that to me, the tugging within my body cavity that I could feel but no longer perceive as pain. I fought back gags as I wiped at my sticky cheeks, the tears still falling despite my want for them to go away. I blinked rapidly, trying to clear them away when the lights of the town approached.

I walked faster, my parent's address burned into my mind as I headed to where I hoped I could call home. I just wanted to be free of the mess of my life. I wanted someone to be there to tell me if it would be okay and actually *mean* it. I wanted my parents, wanted what Jax had talked about, motherly kisses and fatherly hugs. I wanted it so badly it hurt because I knew that it would help heal some of the pain I was in.

Vehicles drove by me but I paid no attention to them as I finally reached the edge of the small town. I practically jogged down the streets trying to find the right one and when I did I frantically read house numbers, my heart in my throat as I drew closer and closer to where they lived.

Finally I stopped in front of a nice and clean yard and a happy looking house. The moon bathed it in moonlight and with my heart in my throat I slowly move up the walkway and to the front door.

My hands shook and my stomach twisted up in knots as I reached for the door. In a moment of panic I felt the sudden urge to turn and run away, terrified at what I would find behind the door but I pushed through it and knocked loudly.

The sound seemed to hang in the air and after a few moments I knocked again. The house was dark but after another few knocks a light turned on and the door was unlocked. I held my breath as it was yanked open and a man with a scowl stared at me.

I didn't know what to say to him and his eyes slowly widened as he looked at me. "Ummm.... hi?" I wanted to hit myself for the squeakiness of my voice but he said nothing, not taking his eyes off me as he slowly tuned his head. "My name is Violet. My parent's live here." I looked at him, hope blooming in me as I realized that we looked similar. I had his eye shape, I could see it.

"Honey." He drew the word out and I could hear the sound of someone else coming closer.

"What, Jes?" The voice was clear and feminine and a woman who looked just like me stepped beside him. He was silent and she looked confused as she looked up at him. A flash of gold on her finger showed me that she was married, probably to the man I believed was my father.

"I don't mean to intrude but I think you are my parents." At my voice her gaze snapped to me and her eyes widened, her face going as pale as her husband's as she looked at me. I went to repeat myself when her eyes narrowed and she grabbed my arm in a tight grip and yanked me into the house.

"*What* are you doing here?" Her words were an angry hiss as she squeezed my arm.

"Irma told me where you lived and I was-"

"You aren't supposed to be here." She cut me off as she said it, looking me up and down as she pulled me further into the house.

I felt utterly confused, this was now how I expected our reunion to go. "I don't understa-"

"Jes, make the call before she thinks we took her and tries to rampage through our house." Her words were sharp and the man moved away. I tried to tug my arm out of the borderline painful grip the woman had it in and she yanked on it hard. "Why *the hell* are you here?" She stuck her finger in my face, her expression twisted with anger.

"I got out of the shop and I wanted to see you." The words seemed childish and stupid even to my own ears and she let me go, wiping her hand on her robe as if touching me made her feel dirty. "You're my mothe-" She whirled around at that, slapping me sharply. I inhaled deeply, shocked by the action as I touched the stinging spot.

"I'm *not* your mother." The words hurt as she flung them at me. "You need to get that through your skull. I might have birthed you but you're Irma's property and I have no investment within you other than a means to an end." Each words was foul and cruel and reinforced everything Irma had ever told me about my parents.

My bottom lip trembled and I looked at her. "I don't understand." I didn't understand it. How had Irma been telling the truth?

Her eyes were hard as she looked at me without an ounce of affection or love. "You were the price of my freedom from that bitch and it was a price I was *happy* to pay."

My heart cracked beneath my ribs, seeping bitter pain into my chest at her callous words. "But-"

She shoved her hand over my mouth, squeezing my jaw and my cheeks tightly. "You will say *nothing* and when Irma comes to pick you up you will tell her you wandered off and that we had *nothing* to do with your escape." She shoved me away and I blinked back tears as I looked at the woman I should have called mother.

"Why are you so horrible?" I asked it quietly, unable to look at her face and not utterly break down and cry.

"Horrible? You think *I'm* horrible?" She gave a short and cruel laugh. "Horrible is being tied to that bitch. I *did* my time."

Anger rose up swift and sharp within me at her words. "And forced the rest onto your very own flesh and blood. Some fucking mother you are." I looked at her, glowering at her darkly as a strange feeling of feral rage rose up in me. "I hope it was worth the price you paid because when you die, you will be judged by the creation for what you have done and you will reap it back tenfold you stupid, horrible cunt." The words flowed through me and she didn't even flinch, just held up her chin and looked down upon me.

"Thanks for the gift of life to be forced to clean up *your* fucking mess." I couldn't believe it. Out of every cruel and heinous thing to do, I was born simply to pay off a debt. Give Irma a new toy to play with so that she could go on with her life with some *human*.

"You have *no* idea what I went through with her." She hissed the words at me, her eye narrowing and it was my turn to give a cold bark of laughter.

"I don't? I have only spent the last twenty six *years* with her, having her experiment on me, torment me, and brutalize me, but you are right. I have *no* fucking idea what she could have possibly done to you. *Absolutely none.*" I couldn't fucking *believe* her. Here was the woman who had grown me within herself, had nurtured me within herself, and birthed me and she was telling me that I had no clue what Irma was like after she *left* me with the cruel witch. She was fucking delusional.

"So fucking dramatic." She crossed her arms over her chest and gave a flippant gesture at me. "I had a life before I was sent to Coven Thirteen, you have never known life without her."

I inhaled sharply at that, rage roaring through me. "And that makes it okay?" My loud voice echoed through the kitchen. "Do you know what I have had to endure in her care? Do you?" At her silence I looked around, spying a knife block. Thar feral rage guided me to show her exactly what horrors Irma inflicted upon me.

"Let me fucking *show* you." I stormed over to the knife block and grabbed the butcher's knife before whirling around and pressing it to where my heart beat in my rib cage. Its beat was hard and heavy with the anger that coursed through me, that hazed my mind. I couldn't *believe* her.

Her arms fell from her chest and she looked at the knife warily. "What are you doing?"

"Do you know what it's like to die?" I shoved the knife in deep, piercing my heart dead on as I slide the blade between my two ribs. The pain was fleeting, the rage burning it away. "Because I fucking do." I gritted the words as she gave a horrified sound, covering her mouth with her hands.

The rage that flowed though me dulled the pain more as I yanked the knife out. The feeling of knife scraping bone making me shudder. Blood immediately started pouring from the wound and my vision flickered rapidly. Weakness encased my limbs and the knife dropped from limp fingers as I collapsed onto the floor.

I was faintly aware of frantic voices as I faded so quickly. I liked this death, it didn't hurt me as much. Didn't make me feel as cold. I was simply... *gone*.

I wasn't sure how long I was out before I inhaled sharply, coughing viciously as my lungs started working, gulping in air greedily. Someone was holding me and a loud voice thundered in my sensitive ears. I shoved at the person, blinking rapidly as my vision slowly came into focus. My body felt funny and off but not nearly as badly as my previously brutal deaths. I preferred it. At least I went down on my own terms.

"What the fuck is happening, Mary?" The man's voice was frantic and I shoved away from him, opening my eyes to a tile floor covered in red. My blood was smeared across tiles and it coated the front of my shirt. The kitchen looked like a brutal murder scene and I wanted to smirk. They deserved to have their pristine and perfect life distorted and coated in the blood of the debt they had settled.

"I don't know!" At the woman's hysterical pitch I tried hard to stand on shaky legs that were unwilling to hold my weight. The man grabbed at me and I slapped his hands away. I didn't want his help. I didn't want either of them to help. "How is she alive?" That hysterical edge was piercing to my brain. It made me wince as I used the cupboard to pull myself to standing and I blinked at the counter top, trying to settle my vision so I wasn't seeing double.

"Shut the fuck up." I ground the words out as I finally looked up at my mother. I didn't care anymore. I didn't. I was done, through. Irma had been sadly right and my mother was nothing but a cruel woman capable of the unthinkable.

"Look at this." At Irma's voice I shuddered and the kitchen immediately fell silent. My father scrambled to his feet, blood smeared across his hands and clothes as he moved towards my mother as if to protect her. "What happened here?" Her tone held a fake note of concern and I turned to look at her. She was tapping one gnarly finger against her lips.

"Looks like your *precious* little bundle of joy showed you my creation." She moved over to me, stroking my cheek with the back of her fingers. I shuddered underneath the touch. "Flawless, isn't it? Time check spell. Keeps her alive no matter how many times she might stab herself in the heart... or have a werewolf rip it out." I winced at that, staring at the counter top once more before I glanced up towards the people who created me.

The man shook his head, disgust painting his features as he gestured to the Elder Witch. "Listen, we agreed to let you have her but that is *not* ok-"

Irma slashed her hand towards him and his mouth shut with a snap. "Shut your mouth, human."

She grabbed my arm in a tight grip. "You gave her to me. I do whatever I *damn* well wish to her. She is *my* property. You have *no* say in her life. Thank your pretty little wife for that." I looked towards my mother and she crossed her arms over her chest once more, staring at the floor off to the side. "I will say that she has grown to look a lot like you, Mary. Nearly identical to you. Pretty too, isn't she?" She grabbed my jaw and squeezed as she jerked my head to the side. I glowered at my mother, daring her to look up and see what she had done to me.

"I think my newest captive will enjoy her... *thoroughly.*" She gave a small cackle at the words and the sound made my blood run cold.

My mother finally caved, looking at Irma. "What are you going to do?" My mother's voice shook slightly and I wanted to bare my teeth at it. She had *no* right to act like she cared about me. She had no right to pretend that she was horrified. She knew what Irma was like when she handed me over as an infant, she had no free pass.

"That is none of your concern but take a good long look at your magick soul, Mary, because this is the last time you will see it so pretty and full of life." Irma patted my cheek roughly as she let my cheek go. "We are going to go. I am sure my prisoner is just *aching* for some company right now." She gave another short cackle before she stopped and pretended to ponder for a moment.

"Well it's no fun if I don't do this first." She smacked my thigh and a heavy burning spread over the spot, wrapping around my leg as poison green runes were pulled into the air.

My mother inhaled sharply. "*Don't*!" At the heavy cry, Irma gave a wide grin, showing off her crooked and yellow teeth before the runes turned to dust and the magick died. I felt no different with it gone and I was confused as to what that meant.

"*Much* better. This makes her so much more useful to me and I think he will find her *much* more appealing now, don't you, Mary?" The question was asked with a heavy does of amusement and I stared at my mother hard. She met my gaze before she looked down at the floor, her shoulders slumping.

"What did you do?" I looked up at Irma and as sickly sweet smile split her face.

"I took off your contraceptive spell." She patted the top of my head in a mocking fashion before turning to Mary. "I think its time you gave your mother some grandbabies." The words were smug and mocking and I felt my stomach sink. "To make her even *more* happy, they are going to be little half-breeds. I need to study the little abominations" At that I felt a bit numb even as my stomach twisted. Babies with a werewolf. I didn't know how to react to that, didn't know if I had the words to even described how I felt. Irma was going to force me to have babies and then take them away. Hurt them. Bile rose up in my throat slowly at the thought.

"Wouldn't you like that, Mary? Your daughter *defiled* by a werewolf, impregnated with the seed of a *beast.*" The words were said nastily and I blinked slowly. "Just remember, when you are trying to sleep at night, her screams will echo in the Coven's halls as the beast has his way with her and remember that it's *all... your... fault.*" Irma gave another spine chilling laugh before the feeling of moving very rapidly hit me and without warning we were sucked through a jump spell and were suddenly in Irma's office.

She let me go, clapping her hands together before shooting a spell at me that seized my muscles and made me drop to the floor as pain roared through me. She held it on me for what felt like ages and my vision went white at the pain. She let it up and I gasped for air.

"That is for escaping." She hit me with another one and I gave a heavy cry of pain as it rolled over me, unable to hold it in. I wanted to thrash, to move because of the pain but I knew it would only make it worse.

After several moments she let it up. "That was for going to your parents." I trembled and gulped in the air I needed to breath, barely aware of her moving towards me. Without warning her foot connected with my stomach, knocking the air out of my lungs and causing me to retch heavily. "That was for showing them the time check spell." She didn't give me time to recover as she buried her hand in my hair, lifting me off the floor.

I grabbed her hand, trying to save my hair as she dragged me through the halls. I struggled to not cry as she twisted her hand viciously, pulling out hair at the roots from my scalp. I bit my tongue to hide the pain as we descended down her tower and towards the dungeons. My heart beat heavily in my chest and bile touched the back of my throat as fear made its presence known once more. It settled around me in a familiar way and I bit my lip hard as she finally stopped in front of one of the cell doors.

Without warning she yanked off my bloody shirt, the buttons popping off as she stripped it from me. She let go of my hair as she viciously removed the rest of my clothes. The cell door responded as she moved closer, opening into the darkness of the cell.

She grabbed my arm and drug me behind her into the dark depths of the cell.

"This is for being nothing but a *waste* of a witch." She hissed the words at me before shoving me into the darkness. I stumbled and landed hard, my knees and hands scrapping against the stone of the cell floor. "Get her pregnant, mutt, and I just might let you go." She laughed, the sound echoed around me but all I could focus on was a low rumbling growl that came from the corner of the cell.

"*Gladly*, you old bitch." The words were growled out and my heart stopped as something moved along the stone towards me.

Chapter Sixteen
Uncovered Truths

She's gone.

It was the only thought that radiated through my chest and stomach when I had awoken. Violet was gone. I had searched the woods, trying to see if she had just wandered off but I hadn't been able to find her. I felt angry as my instinct seethed at me. It wanted us to find the female, to punish her for wandering off. I didn't understand why she would wander off, why she would walk off into the Forest that scared her.

I made my way back to the campsite, I hadn't been able to scent her out, too many animals had been wandering around and her scent was stale. However there was the faint niggling in the back of my mind, she had been focused on Havenbrook.

I didn't understand why she had been so focused on it but I knew that was the best possible lead I had for finding her. I tilted my head, cracking my neck as I thought about how I would punish the little female for leaving without saying a word.

I stalked through the trees, heading towards the highway. My focus was intent on finding Violet. She was going to be punished for making me worried, making me waste time looking for her. I didn't understand her behaviour, didn't understand why everything changed after that mysterious incident that left her cold and covered in blood. I didn't understand what happened and she refused to tell me what happened.

The road came into view and I caught the faint scent of Violet on the breeze and I inhaled deeply, bringing her scent into my lungs. My hunch was right, she had headed for the town. I bared my teeth in anger and moved along the highway towards the town. I wondered if she went there to be with witches... to *escape* me. She hadn't seemed to be as comfortable with me after I came back to her and I wondered if whatever happened to her was the catalyst for her feeling as though I wasn't safe anymore.

It didn't take me long to make it into the town and despite the scents of fuel and exhaust I still had track of Violet's scent. I followed it into the residential area and it grew thicker, less scents covered it up. I could see the humans hurrying towards their homes, their eyes looking over at me as they did so. I bared my teeth and followed her scent right up to the front door of a house.

I thumped hard on the door, banging on it loudly. I could hear shouting from inside before the door was yanked open. "What the hel-" I shoved the man inside the house, growling heavily as I looked at him, grabbing him by his shirt and hauling him upwards.

"Where is she?" I looked around for Violet but there was no sign of her until a woman ran around a corner towards us. She was nearly a carbon copy of the little pixie and I frowned as I let the male drop. Her parents. She had gone to her parents.

"Who are you?" The female hurried over to the man and I couldn't feel magick on her so I was confused. If she was human than how could she have been Violet's mother.

"Where is she?" I stared at her hard, she looked *just* like the little pixie.

Her hands fluttered around the male before she looked up at me. "Who?" She looked as confused as I felt and I bared my teeth at her, letting out a heavy growl.

"The little pixie." I loomed over her and she cowered into the ground, wrapping her arms around the male as he held her just as tightly

" *Who?*" Her voice wavered and I clenched my hands into fists.

" *Violet.* Yer daughter." I couldn't understand how she didn't know who I was talking about. Violet was *clearly* her child.

She looked away, her jaw ticking. "I don't have a daughter named Violet." I felt anger rise up in my thick and heavy. I couldn't understand how a mother would deny her own child.

"Aye, ye do. Ye look jus' like-" I inhaled deeply and stilled. My instinct froze and then roared to life as the scent of the wanted Elder witch filled my lungs. My instinct scraped along my bones and hooked my veins as it moved through me.

Find her

I couldn't agree more with it as I turned on the female, grabbing her throat and lifting her up. "The Elder witch, where is she?" She gasped, grabbing at my arm as she dangled over the floor.

"Don't know." She rasped it out and the male jumped to his feet, attempting to take a swing at me. I dropped the female and dodged the weak hit before I lashed out with my fist, slamming it into his face. He immediately went down and the female screamed, grabbing at his form. I grabbed the back of her neck and crouched down beside her.

"I will kill ye if ye doona tell me where she is." I pressed my claws into the soft flesh, reminding her of who held her life at the moment. "Jus' tell me where she is an' I will not hurt ye." I didn't wish to hurt a female but one who denied her daughter and was lying? I could make a fucking exception.

"I don't *know.*" The words were clipped but I could hear the lie.

"Somethin' tells me not t' believe you." I tightened my grip on the back of her neck, pressing my claws tighter to her skin. "Doona make me hurt ye. Jus' tell me where Coven Thirteen is." She was silent and I lifted up on my grip and she gave a cry, grabbing my hand. "Doona make me, female." She trembled in my grip as her nails scratched at my hand.

"I don't k-" I squeezed forcing her to give another cry of pain.

"Aye, ye do." I pushed against my instinct to cause her even more pain until she sung the information I needed. "Ye don't want me t' be angry but I will get angry if ye doona tell me." I lifted her up more causing another cry to escape her as I forced her to look at me.

"I have killed males for less than a lie. It wouldna take me much t' kill a mother unwillin' t' save her daughter." I was positive that Irma now held Violet, that somehow the witch had gotten her back and I had a very big suspicion it had to do with the two people I was crouched in front of.

"You don't understand." She looked at me, pinching her mouth closed and I blinked at her as I came closer, baring my teeth and snapping them in her face.

"I understand tha' a mother should *never* let her child go for anythin' an' ye failed her." That was worth more than death in my eyes. She needed to be punished and my instinct lashed out at me.

Hurt her for it

I wanted too. I truly did. Wanted to feel her dying beneath my claws and my teeth for what she had done. To betray her own daughter, to hand her over to be tormented. There was no punishment great enough for that.

"Why do you care?" Her chin trembled and her eyes shined with tears.

"Sweet little female she is. *Lusty.*" I grinned at her, baring my sharp teeth as she paled, swallowing rapidly.

"You can't jus-" I squeezed her neck, breaking her skin and causing her to give another cry that roused the male. He looked confused as blood leaked from his nose and he slowly sat up, looking around.

"Tell me where Coven Thirteen is an' I will let ye go." I stared intently at the female as she whimpered.

"Jesus, Mary! Tell him! It's not worth this." The male scrambled to his feet but didn't try to pry me off his female. I wanted to sneer at that. It was rather pathetic.

"I can't!" She wailed it out, tears falling from her eyes as if that would make me feel pity for her. I felt *nothing* for the female. She was the worst kind of creature. A betraying mother.

"It's sixty miles straight east of the town's center. It's at the edge of the Territories but before the Outer Edges." At the male's words I let the female drop and stood up to my full height.

"Doona try t' alert the witch tha' I am comin'. I will come back for yer whole family if ye do. Not even the babe in the bassinet will be safe." Their faces paled as I looked down at them. I would leave not one soul living in the house if that bitch was told I was coming for her. I would kill them all right down to the children. I didn't care. They would inherit their father's cowardice and their mother's cruelty. It would be a favour for the world to have them all snuffed out.

I turned away and walked out the door. I was just glad that some how the little pixie had gotten all of the good from them and retained none of the bad. I could only imagine how she felt knowing that I had been wrong and Irma had been right. Her parents hadn't wanted her at all.

Kill them all

My instinct was persuasive and it took all the control I had not to do just that.

Chapter Seventeen
Charmer

"You alright there, beautiful?" At the voice I scowled darkly and leaned against the stone wall of the cell as I looked into the dark shadows where the werewolf was sitting.

I gave a shrug. I was so far from alright it wasn't even funny. Irma hadn't lied to me at all. My parents hadn't wanted me, I had been torn to shreds by a werewolf, and lied to by the werewolf I had been fucking. My day was so far from okay it was down right shit.

"You look upset. Do you wish t' talk about it." His voice had a faint accent that was very familiar. Not that I was surprised, he looked very much like Jax when my eyes had adjusted to the dark last night and was actually able to see him.

I closed my eyes. "Why does your brother have a stronger accent than you?" I looked into the shadows where the werewolf sat. His hands were in the light as he rested his arms on his knees.

"You know Jaxton?" His voice had an edge and I nodded. I knew Jaxton very intimately, my cheeks flushing at the thought despite all my want for them not to.

"He kidnapped me. It's probably why I'm now here." Took me out of the world I knew and into something else, he was then going to drop me as if I meant nothing. He was going to leave me to a world I had no clue about. I was absolutely ignorant about any and all things that I would be encountering and he was simply going to drop me when he found his brother.

"He hurt you?" At that I shrugged and a sound of frustration came from him. "Beautiful, let me know if he has." There was an edge to his tone but it wasn't directed at me. It brought me back to when Jax had told me why he started treating me better. I wanted to smirk at that. It seemed like Lyxton was the type of male to kick his brother's ass if he had hurt me. "Has he?" At the repeated question I gave another shrug.

"Not personally." My chest still ached from what he *had* done. Betrayed my trust and left me to die. Whether he meant for me to die or not, it didn't matter.

"What do you mean?" There was a heavy dose of confusion to his voice and I let out a small sigh, shifting in my spot. I tugged the werewolf's shirt further down my legs. He had given it to me shortly after her had told Irma he couldn't perform with an audience and she had wandered off. Once she has gone he had given it with a soft and shushing 'its alright now' before he helped me cover myself.

"Beautiful, don't leave me confused now." At the lightly teasing words I felt a small smile grow on my face before it disappeared just as quickly.

"After promising me he wouldn't let anything hurt me, he left me chained in the forest and another werewolf killed me." There was a tickle in the back of my throat but I hadn't said enough to activate the spell. I was learning how far I could push the spell before it would activate. So far I could say a fair bit with alluding before it got cranky.

There was silence from him and I looked over at him before he shifted so he was in the patch of sunlight. His eyes were just as blue as Jax's and it made my chest hurt. He narrowed them at me slightly.

"Ye aren't dead." He said it as if pointing out the obvious and I scoffed.

"I wonder why that is." I grabbed the coiled up length of chain beside my ankle and threw it into the center of the cell towards him. He reached out and grasped the thin chain, looking it over as if it would tell him what was

"This keeps you from dying?" He looked at me and I shrugged but shook my head. The combination had neutralized the spell. I just had to confuse the spell in order to work around it. "What does tha' mean?" His agitation made his accent thicker and I stared at him, trying to figure out how to explain it without the spell activating.

"It means..." I couldn't figure it out and braced myself. "It may or may not allow me to die." I immediately choked on the last word and struggled to breathe, unable to inhale as the familiar tightness closed around my throat. A warm hand rubbed my back as the werewolf murmured at me to breathe.

After a few moments the tightness eased up and I slumped against the wall, my hands shaking slightly as I inhaled deep lungfuls of musty cell air.

There was a silence that fell and he let out a heavy sigh. He settled back on his heels, tilting his head as he lifted the chain. "You can't tell me what spells are on this chain, can you?" I shrugged at him, keeping his gaze locked with mine. "I understand." He gave a short nod and settled against the wall beside me before he grabbed my feet and tucked them onto his lap.

I frowned at that but my expression immediately disappeared as he slowly started to rub them. That felt damn near orgasmic and I shivered and smiled faintly at the massage. I hadn't been treated like that before. I appreciated it.

"I'm sorry that happened to you, beautiful." His voice was a rumble, not a deep or low as Jax's but it was similar.

I looked up at him, scanning his face. His hair wasn't as long as Jax's nor did he seem as severe. He seemed almost on the verge of a smile rather than a scowl.

"It’s not your fault." It wasn't and I didn't want him to feel like he was responsible for it.

"Still, I'm sorry. Jax isn't... He's not known to think his actions through and people tend to get hurt because of it." He looked at me as he firmly rubbed at me feet, he tilted his head as he looked at me. I was basking in the feeling of my feet being rubbed and I couldn't even sum up enough energy to be embarrassed that I was practically purring.

"Have you never been pampered like this before?" His voice pitched upwards with disbelief and my face immediately flushed hotly as I shook my head. "Why not? You are a *delightful* female!" His eyes crinkled at the corners as he lifted my foot up as he rubbed it. He gave an exaggerated sniff of my foot that made me giggle before he grinned at me. "You smell honeyed and warm and *that* means you deserve all the pampering in the world." He lowered my foot as he gave it a friendly squeeze.

"I didn't have a very good life." It came out without meaning to and he gave a small hum of questioning and I swallowed thickly. "My parents only had me to pay off my mother's debt to Irma. I've been with her since I was an infant." It hurt me to know that Irma had been right. That my mother had been such a cruel creature as to have a baby and simply give it to a horrible witch like Irma.

It made a fierce fire burn deep inside me that any babies I had would be loved and cared for like I had never been. I would love them regardless of everything and that if they were taken away from me, I would fight the very world to get them back. I would destroy the very foundations of this world if Irma thought she could get a hold of them.

"She wasn't nice t' you was she?" He looked at me as he slowly rubbed my foot but I just shook my head in response. I didn't want to get into detail about what Irma did. I had been very good at mentally taking myself away from everything that Irma had done to me. I knew what she did but it was like I could only see it through this haze glass window. It was there but separate from me. I was thankful for that.

"Well, let me make up for her treatment." He let my foot go before grasping my other one. "I have to charm myself underneath that shirt according to that bitch." He gave a heavy chuckle of amusement at that before he winked at me, causing a faint bit of heat to warm up my cheeks.

"You are *very* charming." I had to admit it. He *really* was and I doubted he did it deliberately.

He inclined his head at me, a smirk on his face. "That's the difference between Jaxton and I. I got all the charm. He just growls at everything." It was a very accurate statement and I couldn't help but giggle at it.

"So why do you two sound different?" It had been bothering me since he had spoken. Jax's voice had a *much* thicker accent than his own.

At that he let out a heavy sigh. "When we were just babies, Jax and I created our own twin language. As we grew older the more complex and elaborate it became. It had reached the point where we have a distinct accent that goes along with it." He leaned his head against the stone cell wall, smiling up at the ceiling. "Jax doesn't really like speaking normally. He likes the twin language as his default and I prefer to speak like this. This means he has a heavier accent than me." I didn't quite understand what he was saying.

"A twin language?" It seemed absolutely bizarre to me. Everyone spoke English from what I knew, no one spoke anything different.

"Aye, beautiful. Kind of like your magick language." Lyxton looked at me before narrowing his eyes slightly and saying something in a lilting and rapid language that had me blinking rapidly. "See?" He smiled at me and I didn't know what to do but nod at him in agreement.

"Are you mad at Jaxton? For what he did?" He asked it slowly as he looked at me and I paused before giving a slow nod. I was, I was highly pissed off. He had lied to me to have sex and he was going to abandon me afterwards. Why *wouldn't* I be upset or mad?

"He has his work cut out for him with you, doesn't he?" He chuckled at me as I sniffed and crossed my arms over my chest. It would be a cold day in the human hell before I was not angry at him. He was dense and obtuse and he was oblivious to the world around him. He believed he could say or do anything and everyone would fall into line. I knew it would take more than a few pretty words to convince me of anything now. I wouldn't be as trusting the second go around.

"Well then, beautiful." He patted my feet before lifting them off his lap and heading towards the barred cell window. There was a high pitched whistle from outside but it seemed faint and Lyxton returned it with two short and high bursts before he stuck his hand out of the bars and waved his arm once.

He grinned at me as the sound of a truck engine revving reached my ears before the sound of metal crumpling followed. "I'm going to kill you a witch and get that chain off your foot." There was a strange sound outside of the window and Lyxton reached out of the window, muttering to himself before he threaded a chain through the bars with a loud clanking sound.

"I'll be back to get you. A fertile female like you don't deserve to languish in a cell." He chuckled at me as he blew me a kiss right as the metal bars were torn out the window, he was quick to follow them. I was left blinking at the rather large hole in the top part of the wall.

I honestly didn't know if I wanted to get out or not. The outside world fucking sucked.

Chapter Eighteen

Ding Dong the Witch is Dead

I shoved my way out of the large truck I had drove through the front gate and just ripped cell bars out with. I turned to be greeted by a widely grinning Lyxton. I held out my arms, grinning back at him. He hugged me tight and I thumped him hard on the back before letting him go.

"Let's go kill us a witch." I couldn't help the pleased growl I let out as I turned towards the large and eerie looking fort.

"Aye, brother. Should be fun by all accounts." He sauntered towards the large building and I fell into step beside him as I glanced at him.

"Did the witch try t' have her way with ye? Is tha' why ye are missin' yer shirt?" I shoved at his shoulder and he scoffed and rolled his eyes.

"Told me to have my way with a fertile witch. Something about experimenting with half breeds." He grinned back at me and I rolled my eyes. I didn't believe a word he said.

"Now tha' is somethin' I *don't* believe." Witches weren't fertile or compatible with werewolves. If they were, Violet would have been swollen with my babe by the time I was done with her.

Not that I minded the imagery it gave me. I knew she would look just as perfect and sensual with my babe swollen in her belly as she did now. It was just impossible, scents did not lie. She was not compatible with me.

"Always the doubter, Jax." His attention was pulled to the large doors and I looked that way as well before they were shoved wide open and a handful of witches spilled out, their robes dark as night and the air crackling around them. "Hello, pretties!" Lyxton's tone was sickly sweet as his grin grew sharper and I couldn't help how my smile grew sharper as well. It would feel good to destroy several witches for their treachery and vile actions.

"Leave *now.*" The lead witch's voice boomed out and I let out a bark of laughter that was echoed by Lyxton. We stalked forward without pause as we shifted to our beasts simultaneously. Our roars shook the air as we launched at the witches. Blood sprayed the air and coated our claws and teeth as the witches screamed in agony. Their magick did nothing as they tried to scatter away to get the space needed to use their spells.

It didn't take long to kill them all, granted there were less than half a dozen of them but it was surprisingly lackluster that there wasn't any challenge to it. Lyxton and I both shifted down from the beasts. I looked over at him as I rolled my head on my shoulders, liking how my neck cracked.

"Let's find tha' witch." I stalked towards the open doors of the fort and I could hear Lyxton following.

The building felt wrong, too much dark magick was ingrained into the stone for me to think it felt okay. The place reeked of the foul witch's magick. It made my skin crawl. I could hear ghostly echoes of tormented souls that lingered in the walls.

I sharpened my hearing without thinking, listening for the little pixie that I knew was hidden within the walls. There was nothing but a still silence and the haunted sounds that I knew seeped from the stones.

"Where do ye think tha' bitch is?" I looked at Lyxton and he glanced at me, smirking slightly as he slowly looked around.

"*Probably in her tower like all other crazed witches in fairy tales.*" The language that flowed out of his mouth settled my instinct, hammered it home that he was back, that I had gotten him back. I reached out, grabbing his shoulder in a tight grip before I nodded at him.

"*I have missed you, brother.*" I spoke the familiar tongue and he grinned at me before thumping the back of his hand off my chest.

"*And I have you but we have a witch to kill. Let's kill her before we celebrate.*" His teeth grew pointed and I nodded, allowing him to take the lead. He seemed to wander around but there also seemed to be a purpose to how he moved. I had missed my brother for this exact reason. He was a tracker. Could find anything with his nose and lead me right to it so I didn't dare doubt his movements.

"Come out witchy. I knew ye are here." His voice was mocking before he shot out his fist towards a wall. I braced for the impact but his entire arm sunk deep into the wall before he yanked back. The wizened old female's throat was encased in his large hand as she gasped and struggled for air.

Lyxton sneered down at her as he forced her onto her knees. "Going to ambush us? Attack us with our backs turned? Seems right up your alley ye old hag." He spit the words out and I was surprised. I had never seen him or heard him express such vitriol towards a female before but I put it down to the fact the witch was barely female anymore and she truly deserved her punishment.

"Stupid, mutt." She sputtered the words out as she clawed at his hand as it flexed tighter around her throat. I bared my teeth, I wanted to have my chance at killing her, the unknowns of what she had done to poor Violet were hanging over me.

Avenge female

She will reward us

My instinct rasped the words in my ears and I narrowed my eyes at the Elder witch before I glanced at Lyxton who seemed to be taking great pleasure in denying her air and then letting her gulp it down before once again cutting it off.

"*Let me.*" I wanted to feel her blood flow over my skin as I dug my claws in deep. I had already withheld several deaths from my instinct today and I knew I wouldn’t do it again, not this one.

"*Why? I'm having fun.*" He bared his teeth as he once again cut off her airway, watching her gurgle and struggle with a look of pure glee.

"*I promised someone I would show this witch the brutality of werewolves for what she has done.*" I wanted to draw her death from her slowly and carefully. Wanted to show her just how it felt to be unable to escape while death loomed over her.

Lyxton grabbed her chin with his other hand and lifted her off the ground so that she was eye to eye with him. "My brother wishes to show you the brutality of werewolves. I want to continue to play. I'll give ye a choice. Which one of us do ye want to kill ye." I watched the witch as Lyxton grabbed a handful of her hair and let her throat go.

She spat words at us, magick crackling in the air and he immediately clamped his hand over her mouth. "Tsk tsk, so rude." He looked at me before shrugging and making one sharp movement with his hand. There was a cracking sound and the female went limp as her eyes darted around frantically.

"There, I pinched your nerve, now you can't move or cast your magick but you will feel *everything.*" He grinned down at her before letting her crumple to the floor in a heap.

"After you." He gestured for me and I grinned wide as I stalked towards her, my claws pushing out of my nail beds as I reached for her. How I would *enjoy* making her suffer. My claws sunk in deep to her belly and a piercing scream escaped her throat. Lyxton chuckled at it before he crouched down and grabbed one of her limp arms.

I drew my claws through her belly, carving through her flesh like paper as she screamed and cried. It felt good to harm her, to draw the screams out of her throat. A snapping sound had me looking towards Lyxton who was slowly breaking her fingers. I grinned at him and he returned one to me before gesturing lazily at her as if reminding me of my task.

I peeled back her flesh, exposing her organs and her bones. I snapped all the bones I could get a grip on, enjoying the agonized sounds she made. I wondered just how many times the little witchling had made those same sounds and how many times this bitch had gloated over it. The thought made my bare my teeth as I started to pull her organs out, one at a time. Blood stuck to my skin coating me thoroughly as I eviscerated her.

I went to land the finishing blow of removing her frantically beating heart when Lyxton stopped me. I snapped my teeth at him, furious at him stopping me but he merely pointed to a wall where the edges flickered with the dying witch's power.

"Can smell water, wash off the blood." He shooed me away, not letting me close to her nearly dead form and I bared my teeth but stalked towards the wall like he had said.

I stepped through the illusion wall and was greeted by several large barrels of rain water next to a rain catchment system that extended out the window. I walked over to the closest one and shoved my hands into it, splashing water over my chest and my face, wiping away the heated and sticky blood.

I didn't want to clean it off but I also knew why Lyxton had demanded it of me. We had to get rid of the evidence, the scent of blood would lead potential trackers straight to us and we didn't need them finding our hunting grounds.

Find female

My instinct was insistent as I rubbed at my face. I tried hard to shake it off but I knew it was right. We couldn't leave the little female locked up, we would find her and set her free to live her life as she wished. I dunked my head in the barrel, quickly washing the blood out of my hair. As I did so the sound of Lyxton washing up started. I ignored it as I pulled my head from the water, satisfied that I was clean.

"We can go home." Lyxton let out a heavy sigh and I nodded, giving a small grunt as I leaned against the barrel, staring at my reflection. I wasn't one to ponder but my thoughts kept flashing towards the innocent little witch. It wasn't right to leave her here.

"Gotta find somethin' first." I would track her down and pull her from whatever hell hole the witch had her in. Lyxton didn't seem to care as he waved me off, splashing water over his blood soaked face.

I walked away from the rain catchment room, stepping over the brutalized body of the witch, and heading down the hallways, shoving doors open as I did so. I made it through several rooms without finding the witchling until I stumbled upon one with clothes.

My boots and clothes were in the courtyards, destroyed from the shift. I yanked several pieces of clothes from the pile, pulling them on, ignoring how tightly they fit over my chest. They were obviously designed for some weak warlock. I sneered at that before grabbing a set of boots, shoving my feet into them before gathering up a quick outfit for Lyxton.

I came out of the room right as he was walking passed. I shoved the clothes as him and he took them with a nod. I continued my search, growing more and more irritated by the lack of the little female.

I bared my teeth angrily, I couldn't even scent her out and I knew it had to do with the magick that was slowly leaving the walls. She was hidden and I knew it would take more than me to find her. I turned for the main doors, I would recruit Lyxton to help in my search.

I nodded at that and stalked out of the fort, looking for him. I spotted him by the busted open cell. He was crouched down beside the opening and I moved towards him, curious as to what he had. He stuck his arms into the hole as I drew closer and without any effort he pulled someone out.

Pale and delicate arms were the first thing I saw before dark hair and a pale figure wrapped up in a plaid button up followed. The little female tucked her hair behind her ear and I realized it was Violet.

Lyxton squeezed her shoulder, smiling at her widely as the little chain slid off of her ankle and turned to ash. Anger flared in my belly as I drew closer and realized Lyxton's scent coated her thickly. I bared my teeth, a deep and dominating growl escaping my throat as I reached them. I reached for her but without warning the little female whirled around.

There was a crackle of heavy magick in the air as the back of her hand connected with my cheek and sent me flying into the side of the fort. I slammed into it feeling like I had been hit by a truck. I hit the ground hard and I felt dazed as I got to my feet, shaking my head to clear the dizziness away.

"Back *off.*" Her little face was twisted with anger and her brown eyes flashed with it.

Punish female

My instinct shoved at me hard as I growled and moved towards her once more. She raised her hand in warning and I snapped out my own, grabbing her wrist in my grip tightly before pushing her again the wall. I was filled with anger and rage and pride that the little witch had grown claws. I grinned at her as she struggled against my grip, glowering up at me.

"Let go of me!" She kicked out at me and I grabbed her leg, holding it behind the back of her knee before I hooked it over my hip and kissed her hard.

Our teeth clicked together from the force and I liked that. I wanted it to be bruising and dominating. I wanted her to feel claimed by me, to feel like *I* was the only male that she would *ever* let between her thighs. My anger burned in me just as strongly as the desire but it was soon replaced with a stillness as I took in her scent. Clean, pure, and feminine. I waited for that bitter undertone but instead her scent grew warmer, *sweeter.*

Ferrrrrrrtiiilllllle

I shuddered as my instinct raked the word down my spine. The little female was *compatible* with me. I kissed her a bit more frantically and she wasn't telling me to back off with how her sharp little nails dug into me and her lips moved on mine as she twirled her tongue around my own.

I reached down, grabbing her other leg and hoisting her up so I could settle in the cradle of her hips where I was meant to be. She was *fertile* and *willing.* I wanted to plant my seed in deep so no other male would attempt to take her away from me.

"Don't want to interrupt but ummm *mixed company.*" Lyxton's voice pierced through to my head and I pulled away from the little pixie to glower at him as a heavy growl escaped my chest. He shrugged, a smirk teasing the corner of his mouth as he looked between the two of us. "*If you aren't will to share, brother, get a room.*" I couldn't ignore the blatant look of appreciation he gave *my* little pixie as she tried to tug me back into the kiss.

I shifted so he couldn't see her as I bared my teeth, feeling angry and unbalanced at his interest.

"*Mine.*" The words was guttural no matter the language I spoke it but it just made Lyxton laugh.

"*Let's let the little female choose, brother.*" He looked me up and down, that smirk finally emerging. A snarl escaped me that had him laughing all over again as stinging pain followed my agitated little pixie's nails as she demanded I return to her mouth. There would be no way she would choose Lyxton. I held the knowledge to pleasure her how she liked and Lyxton would *never* match me.

Chapter Nineteen
Angry Magick

I walked beside Lyxton, looking around the forest. "So can the trees really get that big?" I looked up at him and he nodded.

"Aye, as big around as a truck." He looked down at me before smirking and lifting an arm and flexing his bicep. "Not nearly as big as *me* though." At that I couldn't help but laugh. He was a funny male, I liked that. I grinned up at him and he reached out, pulling me to his side as he gave me a hug. "You know jus' how to make a male feel better about his freedom." He let me go and I smiled, he was very easy to get along with.

A muttering from behind us made me scowl. Jax was glaring at us, I could feel the angry gaze on my back and while it made me want to cower slightly, it made my unfamiliar magick roll through my veins rather angrily. It was strange for me to feel it, to have a connection to something that was so... *alien* to me.

I knew that I had the magick since I had been born, I had been my mother's magick soul. I was her transition from witch to human, I *was* her magick but the fact it had been barred from me since birth made it feel strange within me.

It felt like a living entity within me and it felt just so... *odd.* However in this instance it matched how I felt. I was angry and upset with him. He had no rights to be upset with me. He had wronged *me*, I had done *nothing* to him.

Lyxton bent down, his head close to mine. "Don't worry, beautiful. He's just jealous." He winked at me and there was a low and rumbling growl that made him chuckle. "See?" He rubbed my back and I rolled my eyes as Jax let out another heavy growl.

His glower was intense and pointed and it made me shiver slightly. Lyxton just let out another chuckle. "Nothing has ever come between us before, beautiful. I must say tha' I never expected it to be such a *lovely* female." His words were low and amused and I blushed heavily at that, reaching up and pressing the back of my hand to my heated cheeks as he rested his hand on my lower back.

"You should see my cabin, beautiful. Its very spacious. *Perfect* for children." He said the words loud enough that I knew Jax could hear them and his glare grew more heated against my back.

I picked up on what Lyxton was doing and I grinned up at him. "Is it?" I wanted to needle Jax, wanted to poke and prod at him. He had hurt me and I wanted to get back at him. It didn't matter that he could kiss me until I forgot the world around me. It didn't matter that he was the first and only male that had cared about *my* pleasure. It didn't matter that his touch made me melt.

What mattered was the fact he had lied to me to have sex, that he wanted to abandon me to a world I didn't know or understand.

I had a suspicion that the only reason I was with them now was that Lyxton had taken pity on me. I wasn't sure if it was because of my shitty childhood or what had happened between me and Jax. I was confused by it and Lyxton wasn't helping that confusion as he rubbed my lower back with a low chuckle.

"I know ye are thinking, beautiful. I wouldn't worry about it. You might enjoy him jealous." He bumped his hip against mine and that dark rumble that followed us grew louder and louder until I was picked up around the waist and thrown over Jax's shoulder.

I let out a sound of indignation, thumping my fist against his back as my magick crackled violently in my veins. His growls were loud and dominating as we moved further away from Lyxton.

"You put me down *right* now!" I bared my teeth as he let out a dangerous snarl, my magick felt unpredictable but just out of my reach. I couldn't get a hold of it like I had the first time I had hit him. It was frustrating me that it was so clear and close but I couldn't touch it. "Right *now*!" I didn't want him to be close enough to me to make me forget about my anger.

He gave another snarl as his long strides took us further and further away before he abruptly stopped and set me down. His grip was tight on my hips before he pulled me close.

"Stop!" I shoved at his chest and it vibrated against my palms as he shoved his face into my neck and the heat of my desire flooded through me.

He spoke roughly in that language, that I knew I would never be able to decipher, as his large hands spread out over my sides before he slid his hands down to grab my ass. I gave a gasp of indignation as he lifted me up.

"You do *not* get to man handle me!" My magick finally sparked from my hands and snapped against his skin as he lowered me down to the ground.

"*Silence.*" It was a deep and heavy order that had me trying to kick him. I wasn't just some dainty little female. I would do my best to hurt him even as I shivered as his hands slid up the skirt I was wearing. I attempted to head butt him and he let out a heavy growl as he looked down at me, his hands holding me tightly.

"He willna *treasure* ye like I do." It was a rumbled and rich statement that made my nipples harden against the plain bra I had been given to wear. I hated that he had that much control over my body using just words.

"Fucking *liar*!" I hated that he was giving me sweet words in an attempt to get me to spread my legs for him. I hated that I was still nothing more to him than a willing female. However it was getting harder to fight when I knew boundless pleasure for me rested in his hands.

He pressed his mouth to my neck and I inhaled sharply. "He willna *cherish* ye like I do." He muttered the words against my skin and I bared my teeth, scratching my nails over the back of his neck as he grunted a sound of appreciation.

"*Lies.*" He would continue to lie to me until he decided he was done with me and I would be left alone. I didn't *want* that. I wanted a guy to *love* me and all I had was a horny werewolf who was making my mind hazy with desire. I wanted to shove him off because of my anger but I was also throbbing for him, my sex was practically weeping for him.

I pushed his head from my neck and he relented after a few moments. I pulled him down, pressing my lips against his. Despite his lies I still liked how the sex made me feel close to him. I also liked sex with him period and if he was offering I wasn't going to reject that. I slid my legs apart and allowed him to press between them as I tangled my hands into his long hair.

He took control immediately and both of our actions were frantic and borderline angry as clothes came off, nearly tearing before we were both naked and he slid deep within me. My back arched and I let out a drawn out moan as I drug my nails over his shoulders.

"Fuckin' *exquisite.*" He bit my neck as he thrust into me. My mouth dropped open and my eyes fell closed as I panted, matching his movements with my own. "Do ye like this?" At the rough growl as he slid his hand down my side to grasp my ass and giving it a heavy squeeze as he gave a hard thrust. I moaned in response, giving a faint nod.

I couldn't speak, too focused on chasing that peak to say anything. That slick heat that was rolling over me as my neck and chest flushed with my pleasure and desire. His mouth closed over one nipple and a harsh exhale escaped me at the pleasure that it brought. I writhed beneath him, unable to think as his movements grew harsher, angrier. He pulled his mouth away from my aching breast as he removed his hand from my ass and sunk it into my hair.

"Feel what I do t' ye, Violet." His voice was rough and guttural as he thrust into me again and again, shoving me up towards that peak, heating my body so that sweat beaded on my skin. "He will *never* make ye feel this way. *Never.*" At that roughly said word I shattered around him, bathing him in my release as I gave a sharp cry as the pleasure crashed over me in waves that made my skin tingle and my body convulse slightly.

He bit my neck, giving a heavy and possessive growl as he gave a heavy thrust, unleashing within me and leaving me feeling almost claimed by the wicked and torturous weremale. My arms fell over my head, breathing heavy as he made his temporary claim over me and my pleasure and there was a small spark of fear within me that he was right.

There would be no other male that would make me feel the way he did.

Chapter Twenty

Revelations and Promises

She was ignoring me still. I controlled her pleasure, made her see stars and the heavens but once she came down from those heights she was icy and cold towards me. I hated that she was showing her preference to Lyxton over me. He made her laugh and smile and she refused to give those warm looks to me. I looked for her in the Forest, she was gathering herbs for Lyxton, barely looking at me unless she was scowling darkly.

He looked proud of himself and I bared my teeth in agitation. I didn't understand how the female could moan out my name as I took her to heights I knew no other had ever taken her, only to shut me out during the day like she was.

We were growing closer and closer to our hunting grounds and the time for her to choose was growing slimmer and Lyxton simply smirked at me, laughing as she continually approached him over me. I drew her into my arms nightly, showing her again and again that no one could make her feel as I did yet she continually denied me.

Take female

Claim her

Breed her

My instinct hounded me constantly. I wanted to place my babe within her so she couldn't leave me but I knew my own limits with her and how females could see that deception. Lyxton approached me and I couldn't help the warning growl I gave out. Some how the little female had stuck herself between me and my brother, dividing us. I didn't like but I couldn't control how I felt. I had found her first, I had made my claim on her and Lxyton was a threat to that claim over the fertile female.

"Easy, brother. Always so serious." His mouth twitched upwards as he looked at me and I glowered at him, unable to find his ease with the situation. He settled in to stand beside me and it took everything I had not to lash out at him like my instinct demanded. Its whispers were insidious.

Remove competition

Take female for self

It repeated over and over again as it mixed with its pushes to claim the little pixie and ensure a babe rested deep in her belly. I bared my teeth, my gaze landing on her. She was elegant and beautiful and I was satisfied with the fact she was the one who would bear my young. I had refused to allow such thoughts before but scents did not lie and she was now highly compatible with me. Her scent growing more and more sweet and warm the longer I was around her. It was enough to drive a male mad with his desire to claim.

"She's a beautiful female, isn't she?" Lyxton was looking at me but I refused to meet his gaze, an unwanted growl building in my chest at his appreciation for the creature my instinct and I had deemed was our own. *"No need to reply to me, its painted all over your face."* He gave a chuckle at that and it had me bristling angrily. I didn't like being so transparent but I had to calm myself down with the reminder that he was my twin and he saw through everything I tried to hide.

"She likes me. Sweet little thing." He said it offhandedly and I snapped my teeth with aggression, whirling around to hit him but he simply deflected the hit and tripped me, sending me to the ground with ease.

I sputtered with anger, hating that I had fallen for that stupid trick. I shoved against the ground and Lyxton let out a heavy sigh. *"You are **so** stupid."* He reached down and yanked me back to my feet. *"Letting anger guide you. Mama always said you were the act first think second child."* He brushed me off, ignoring my agitated movements to get him to let me go. *"That female prefers me to you for **one** reason."* He let me go and I shook myself off, glaring at him darkly. He didn't see to care about that as he rolled his eyes. *"She is upset with you, brother."* He said it like I hadn't already guessed it and I scoffed.

*"I noticed that. I'm not **blind**."* I didn't like him insinuating that I was. My gaze flickered to the little female who was sitting down, scanning the herbs in her lap as if trying to figure out which one was which.

*"I never said you were but you **are** stupid. Do you know **why** she is upset with you?"* He looked at

me as if expecting an answer and I just shrugged, shaking my head. I had no clue why she could be so upset with me. I knew nothing of the little female and it was something that was growing more and more agitating for me. If I didn't know her then I could not possibly make her want pups with me like I needed to. *"When you left her in the Forest she got hurt, **badly**. You promised her she wouldn't be hurt in your care and she was."* The images of her covered in blood, cold and pale flashed through my mind and guilt ate away at my stomach like a strong acid.

"She feels as though you said those things to get between her legs and while I see the point of her argument I know that my brother would not lie about protecting someone. Not for that." He looked at me carefully. *"That is not the brother I know."*

He said his last sentence but I was already stalking towards the little pixie. If that was why she was upset with me then I would right the wrong. I hated that she had been hurt and it was my fault. I never wanted her hurt or harmed, I would never wish for that. Her head jerked up and her eyes narrowed as she caught sight of me but her unreliable magick did little but spark at me as I picked her up carrying her away from my brother for privacy.

She struggled, cursing at me and her magick as she struggled in my grip, fighting to escape. I ignored it, even when she hand slapped me upside the head several times and she pinched my ear hard.

I abruptly set her down when I felt we had gone far enough away and she was fuming, her face red and her brown eyes flashing with fire that made me proud. She had grown claws, knew how to use them, and from how she bared her teeth at me with her anger she had found her teeth as well.

"How *dare* you!" She spit the words at me, pressing her hands to her hips as her pixie like face twisted with her anger. I adored seeing her so fiery and upset. I liked a strong female that was not scared to show me she was vexed. "You do *not* ge-"

"I'm sorry, pixie." The words were not hard to say because I was. I had allowed her to get hurt in my care, allowed harm to befall her after I gave her my *word* that I would keep her safe. I knelt in front of her, bowing my head in supplication as I bared my neck to her.

"You think apologizing is going to fix what happened?" Her voice was sharp as if it were coated in thorns and I slowly looked up at her. Her eyes flashed and burned as she looked at me. "You *chained* me to a tree! Left me *alone* and he came and he *killed* me." Her voice was higher pitched and she was breathing heavy. "Do you know how it feels to die? Do you know how it feels to be underneath a spell that can casually allow your death for some perverse sense of *research*?" I didn't have a response as she stormed closer, pointing her finger at me as her chest heaved with her anger.

"Out of *all* of the deaths I have endured over my life, nothing comes close to the brutality of a werewolf. *Nothing*! And you left me out there for one to kill me." There was a sheen to her gaze that had me once again bowing my head. I did not know what she was speaking of but the little witch was not lying. A male had indeed killed her and some how a spell caused her to come back.

"Ye came t' harm under my care an tha' is inexcusable." It was. It would be a burden and a blight upon my soul to have that mark there. I had broken my word to a female I had wished to cherish and please.

"You *lied* to me! Promised me I wouldn't get hurt and told me *all* of these things just to get into my pants and like some stupid *idiot*, I believed you!" The amount of self derision she had set me teeth on edge and I snapped my head up to look at her.

"Nay! Doona *ever* think that I said as I did t' get between yer thighs." I would never promise those things for sex. I would never promise her that. The only promise I would give her for sex would be to promise her that any pups we had would be protected by me completely and totally and that she would be cherished and protected forever more if she made such thoughts realities. "I *doona* promise my protection in exchange for sex, pixie." It was low and cowardly. I wanted to protect her because she was a sweet little female who had *deserved* protection and who had been *scared*.

"Then why did you? *Huh*? You kidnapped me and then promised to protect me. *Why*?" The hurt she felt was now clearly painted across her face and it hurt me to see it, to see that I had caused this divide within her.

"Because I *care* about ye. Do ye na understand this?" It was what a male did when he cared, he made promises. I wondered if this was the showing of just how her life had jaded her, as if I were the straw that broke the poor female's back.

"*Another* lie! You are just going to leave me like you planned." She threw out her arms as she glared at me through tears that wanted to fall as her chest heaved. "Go home with your brother and have your own life, isn't that what you said? Leave me to a world I don't know to just *figure* it out on my own!"

She shouted the words at me and I could finally understand why she was hurt. The little female was scared I would leave her.

I bared my teeth at that, immediately getting to my feet. "Make *no* mistakes, Violet, leavin' ye is the *last* thing on my mind." I stalked towards her, looming over her as I scanned her face. "I am goin' t' put a babe in yer belly and watch ye grow heavy with my child." I pressed my hand to her stomach and she jumped as she looked down at it.

"Ye will be by my side from now till the end an' there will be *nothin'* in this world tha' will tear me away from ye. Understand tha', pixie." I growled the words at her, my instinct thrashing inside of me to show her how I had claimed her above everyone else. I knew that I owned her body and her pleasure but I wanted to claim her mind, to show her that no matter what I would be by her side.

Her hand covered mind and she seemed to sway before she looked up at me, those brown eyes wide with confusion. "You want to have babies with me?" It was such a trembling question that I had to pull her close and tuck her into the safety of my arms.

"As many as ye'll give me, Violet." A pack of little children that would run around their mother as her eyes shined with her love.

"I *want* babies." It was a soft murmur and I nodded, holding her closer.

"Then I can do nothin' but provide what my female wants." And I would for the rest of time. If there was one thing she could count on it was that. She would come first, cherished above all, and I would make up for the years she had suffered under the cruel hands of the witch that had accidentally brought us together.

Epilogue
Happiest of Homes

I hummed as I stoked the fire of the wood burning stove, the cabin was warm and cozy despite the howling winds outside. It felt good to be safe and sound, no worries about food or safety. I was well taken care of in my little pocket of world I had. I moved to check on the roast I had set in the oven for supper and the rich scent of savoury venison and spices wafted into my face as I opened the door. My stomach growled but twisted unpleasantly. It was something I had been trying to get used to.

I pressed my hand to my stomach with a sigh. I wasn't very good at magick, I had years of knowledge I had to acquire and despite Jax and Lyxton finding me all the spell books they could, it was slow going. I was just happy that my earlier spell had worked and it had worked again and again and again. It felt good to use my magick, to feel that part of me no longer be unfamiliar or strange.

I walked over the smooth floorboards and towards the cupboards. Jax had sanded the rough floor down the first day I had come here. I had gotten a splinter from one of them in the bottom of my foot and once he had extracted the sliver from my foot he had set me on the table and ordered me to stay before he sanded down every inch of floor so it was nothing but smooth to the bottoms of my feet.

A faint heat flared in my cheeks as I pulled down a stack of plates and moved over to grab some cutlery. I felt *beyond* pampered by Jax. He was possessive and dominating but nothing was ever done to me without my say so and he made it his focus for me to want for nothing. I hadn't wanted for much, not knowing what luxuries really were ask for them but any little silly thing I wanted, like curtains for the windows or a cheery table cloth for the table, it was acquired for me. So was the area rug and the well worn furniture in the living room.

He had allowed me to make the space my own and it felt like home whenever I came into the space. My gaze slowly moved to the partially made cradle that sat beside Jax's chair. He had set about constructing one when he had gotten me here. Slowly making every spindle and piece by hand. He refused my suggestions that he just find one, telling me that his babes would rest in his love even when far from his arms. It made me melt for the male even more than I already had.

I moved back towards the stove once the cutlery was on the stack of plates, ready for when supper was done. It was dark outside and I knew Jax and Lyxton would be returning shortly. Excitement bloomed up in my chest at the thought.

I stirred the potatoes before poking one with a fork and nodding my head. I carefully pulled the pot off the stove and drained it over the sink before throwing a pat of butter into is and a sprinkle of salt before putting the pot on the table. I moved over to the vegetables and did the same, draining them over the sink and setting the pot on the table.

Everything looked and smelled wonderful and I gave a happy smile. I was turning into quite the little cook. I had been absolutely shit at it until Lyxton had taken me underneath his wing, showing me everything he knew about cooking and helping me when I wavered on somethings, unsure of what to do. He was a very nice male and I hoped he found a female for himself. He truly deserved one.

The door was shoved open, causing me to jump as a rush of bitter winter winds followed the two large males inwards into the warmth of the cabin. "Jax!" I smiled brightly, rushing towards him, leaping into his arms as he laughed, a rich and warm sound that made me feel cherished.

"Aye, pixie, tis me." He held me tight to his chest as he walked further into the house, setting me down only to kiss me long and hard. I swayed towards him, getting lost in the passion he was showing me as he pulled me close, low growls rumbling the air as his heated form chased away the cold the winter had brought into the cabin.

He drew back from the kiss, pulling my head to his chest as he kissed the top of it. "Smells good." His voice rumbled into me and I smiled proudly, holding him just as tightly as he was holding me.

"And tell us how the food smells, Jax." At Lyxton's cheeky response I blushed heavily at the implication and Jax merely laughed as he let me go.

"It smells good as well." He gave my ass a playful swat as he moved to take off his winter gear beside Lyxton. I grinned at the action despite the pink I knew that stained my cheeks at it and I headed back to the stove, opening the oven door.

"Ah ah." Lyxton was immediately beside me, gently and playfully moving me aside. "You have done enough." I stepped back and watched him pull out the roast, inhaling deeply with a faint look on his face. "Ye added juniper this time." He gave me a look and I kind of shrunk in on myself, unsure if it was a good choice but his beaming smile was enough to return my confidence as I nodded.

"Make a world class cook out of ye." He settled the roast on the table beside the other dishes and I quickly moved to grab the dishes. "I suggest my brother puts a babe in your belly before a more handsome male steals ye away." Lyxton winked at me and I flushed even as Jax gave a low warning growl.

I carefully set the plates out, making sure each one had a knife and a fork. My heart hammered in my chest as I slowly finished. "Jax can't put a baby in me right now." At the words both males stilled and looked at me. Jax with heavy confusion and Lyxton with abject curiosity.

"Why do ye say that, beautiful?" He pulled out his chair and settled into place and my mouth felt dry as I wrung my hands in front of me, suddenly nervous.

"I have to have this one first." I pressed my hands to my belly and the growing life that I knew, without a doubt, rested within me. The silence was thick and there was a tense moment before Jax was suddenly by my side.

He hit his knees before moving my hands out of the way and burying his face into my stomach. He inhaled deeply, his hands grasping my hips. I let my hand fall to his shoulders as tears welled in my eyes as he stiffened, pushing closer and inhaling again and then again as it to cement it deep within himself that my scent had indeed changed, no matter how small, and there was a little life growing deep within me.

He yanked me down, pulling me onto his lap as his fingertips brushed my cheeks and my mouth as he held me close. Those blue eyes burned as they looked at me and he closed them pressing his forehead to my temple and cupping my belly.

"A babe." He breathed the words out and I nodded, sniffling. The spell had come back positive every single time I had done it and I had done it repeatedly just to make sure I was doing it perfectly.

"A baby." I was going to have a little baby, a child. I was going to be able to finally make up my childhood by giving another the love I never had growing up. I was going to be able to kiss tiny feet and hands, tickle a tiny belly, and show a little creature that I loved them to the ends of this world and back a hundred times over.

"Ye're *magnificent.*" Jax pressed his lips to my temple. *"Stunning."* His voice grew more soft and carried on low and growled tones. *"Wondrous."* Each word he said he pressed his lips to a new place on me. The shell of my ear, my cheek bone, the side of my nose.

"I will pamper ye endlessly." He held me tighter, his face going to my nec as he held me like he would never let me go again. "Cherish ye with all tha' I am an' will be." His hand smoothed over my belly as my tears started to fell at the endless *love* that I felt emanating from him. This was not the first time I had heard him say those things to me but it was the first with that much apparent love.

"Love ye like *no* male has *ever* loved another." He pulled back, those startling blue eyes shining with joy and happiness and most of all love before brushed his lips against mine. He tucked me close, rocking me as he whispered to me all that he would do for me and all that he would give. He promised me the earth beneath my feet, the stars above my head and everything in between.

I closed my eyes, finally basking in the feeling of being cherish and loved. Jax could promise me anything but there was only one promise I needed from him as I pulled back and looked at him. "Will ever stop loving me?" I met his gaze and it burned so bright and intense I felt like I would be burned.

"*Never.*" It was that rasping whisper and the kiss that followed that cemented my future in front of me. No more uncertainly or fear because my world was completely and utterly set in stone. There was no need for fear because Jax would *always* be right beside me.

Author's Note

Thank you for reading the second instalment of Twisted Dark!

I needed to showcase what was actually happening to Violet and how our perceptions of people and our biases can skew what we know. BamBam saw Violet in a singular way but we can see that she was a product of the life she had been forced into. That she didn't really deserve the torments handed to her.

All in all, I loved writing this story and introducing Jaxton and his slightly wild nature. I hope you join me in reading the next instalment as well!

I hope you guys loved reading this novella just as much as I did writing it.

Until next time

Anna M. L. Koski

Acknowledgements

I want to thank everyone who has believed in me from the start! My readers, my family, my best friends and pf course my twinsie, Ashley. I love you all, from the bottom of my heart.

I would love to once again give my thanks to my readership and community for their unfailing support and appreciation in all that I do in my writing. They are always full of encouragement and happiness and never once let me fall. They have always encouraged me and pushed me to strive for what they believe I can do. I absolutely adore them for that.

I need to acknowledge my family. Even though my niece is still a bit too young to read this book, in my opinion. (If you *are* reading this, AVERT YOUR EYES, CHILD!) She has shown my unfailing support with my writing and reading the stories I let her read. And of course I need to thank my mum for being supportive and letting me bounce ideas and tell her the stories inside my head!

And, as always, my last thank you goes to my twin, my best friend, and my soulmate, Ashley. She and I have been friends for nearly seven years and I couldn't imagine my life without her. She is and always will be my soulmate no matter where life takes us.

So once again, I love you and thank you for being there for me.

About the Author

Anna M. L. Koski grew up on the family homestead in the rolling hills of Southern Saskatchewan. She has always been an avid writer and has a boundless love of literature.

Time has not lessened her desire to write but has only seemed to make her passion for it that much stronger as the years have gone by. You will likely find her staring at her laptop writing page after page of her stories even in the wee hours in the morning.

She has a great love of encouraging others to follow their dreams and to pursue their passions. She believes a life is only well lived if it is lived in happiness and contentment. She lives by her mother's motto and encourages others to do the same.

The tallest trees have the strongest roots.
Never forget where you came from.

Coming Soon

Underneath a Dark Moon

Twisted Dark

Anna M.L. Koski

Introducing the Third book in the Twisted Dark Series!
Underneath a Dark Moon

Read further for sneak peek of the newest instalment!

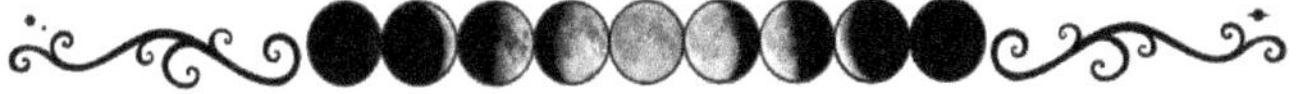

Lacey wasn't a very good witch.

She was born to a powerful witch with a powerful warlock as a father, her siblings were also very powerful, the most powerful of all was BamBam. So in the face of such infamous magick, she had always felt inadequate. She was a Nolo Vis, who called herself Novis, but to everyone else, she was considered just as her magick was. Non-existent.

That all changes when the high Mercutio Anadori, the Warlock King himself, sets his eyes on her. He offers to take her hand in marriage if she helps him find her sister. She had been kidnapped by a rabid werewolf and brainwashed into helping his nefarious purposes. She readily agrees out of love for her sister and the fact that the Warlock King is very sweet and considerate and the unnoticed Lacey is swept off her feet.

So with the promise of marriage from the extremely powerful Warlock King, she starts her search for her sister with a large werewolf named, Abe. He was ordered to protect her but Novis has never encountered a werewolf before and is intimidated by the hulking mass of werewolf that follows her with a still sternness and a crass mouth.

Things start to spiral out of control. Lacey starts to feel a deep attraction to the intense werewolf sent to guard her. He looks at her like no one has before, as if she was something of value and worth that was beautiful to behold. She is stuck between a deadly desire and her promise to King Mercutio for marriage.

But her as body starts to fail on her, and having no magick to speak of, Lacey knows time is running out and that things aren't always what they seem. She begins to wonder who she can trust in a world where enemies are behind every corner. Who is the true enemy, the Warlock King, her sister, or the werewolf who sets her body and imagination on fire?

Hush hush
Let your Magick rush

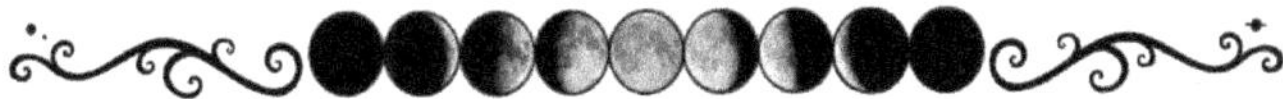

Chapter One

Try Again

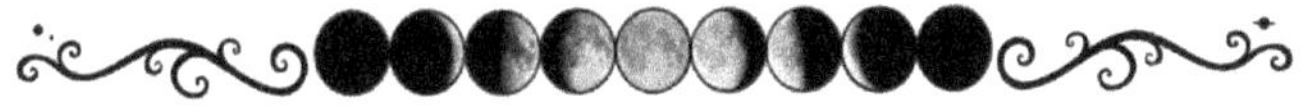

I stared at the dark sheet that hung above the altar, the dark red swirling designs barely cutting through the darkness that lingered in the candle light. My heart beat heavily in my throat as I drew the ever familiar symbol in the air.

"Powers of high, listen to my plea." My voice shook and wavered, the pleading was clear. I wanted this *so* badly it *hurt.* "Three aspects of the Divine, I invoke thee." I lit the pillar candle in front of me, my eyes never leaving the designs I could see. I just wanted them to glow for me, just *once.* "This magick time, this magick hour. I ask you to lend me your power." I drew the symbol again, this time above the lit candle.

"Bless this symbol with your love, bless this symbol with your might, I feel you with me day and night." I did. I felt the magick so tantalizingly close. It was right where I could reach but it always scurried away before I could firmly grasp it. "Hear my call, hear my plea." I wanted to blink, my eye burned but I kept them open. I needed to watch the tapestry, needed to watch for the sign. "Three as One always with me! Three as One forever be!" I inhaled deeply, waiting in anticipation but just like the two thousand, five hundred times before, there was nothing.

I slumped, exhaling my disappointment as I pushed my hood back from my face. Giggling sounded off from behind me but I did my best to ignore it. "Perhaps next time?" I looked up at the tapestry with a hopeful gaze before I straightened and blew out the candle. "Bless you, three Divines, for your patience with me. I will see you tomorrow." I drew the sigil for thankfulness in the smoke from the candle before I stood up, using the altar to pull myself up as my knees groaned their protest. I had been kneeling too long and they were complaining the harshness of the floor. One would have thought I was an old crone rather than merely twenty-six.

"You think she would just stop it. She's Nolo Vis. The Divines won't touch her." The words were a venomous hiss that scraped down my spine and I knew they were loud enough for me to hear but I ignored them, reaching out and brushing my fingers across the tapestry with a touch of longing. BamBam would have turned around and told the two younger witches that they could shove their words up their asses before lighting their robes on fire but I wasn't Bam. Not even close.

I was Lacey 'Novis' Lenkirion, I was a level one witch with barely enough magick to conjure up a candle worth of flame, let alone set someone on fire. Besides I was shy and non-confrontational. The most I confronted people was by going by Novis. Bam told me it was the best way to snub my noses at the bitches who laughed at me and I had to admit that, despite how I *hated* having Nolo Vis hissed at me, it brought me great pleasure to turn around and tell them no, it was Novis.

"Are you going to be done in this century?" At the agitated voice I deliberately moved slower as I picked up my candle and other items. I could feel their agitation rising and I carefully put everything back into my bag before I turned away from the altar. "You would think a Nolo Vis would know where they didn't belong!" The young witch hissed the words at me as she narrowed her eyes darkly.

I fought back my anger at the words and smiled at her. "Novis." I watched as she frowned, as if confused by my reaction.

"What?" Her face twisted up further in agitated confusion. That made me feel a little bit better. One of these times I did the ritual it would come back the way I wanted it too and I wouldn't need to go by Novis, wouldn't need to be hissed at but until then, I would take my little bit of confrontation where I could safely get it.

"Not Nolo Vis. I'm Novis, but I can't see how you would be confused." I smiled at her once more as I moved smoothly by her and her friend. I wouldn't have to see them again after this, they would awaken their magick and go to another coven and a tiny feeling of spite rose up in me. "Perhaps when you get better educated you will come to understand the difference instead of speaking as if you are the coven idiot." The mocking words escaped me and my heart jolted as I hurried away, unwilling to stay and take whatever retaliation that would come from the witch.

A perfect example of why I was nothing like BamBam. She was my big sister and I loved her but she *always* spoiled for a fight and with me, if someone merely raised their voice I felt like crying. I was a mouse, a pushover, a pansy. There was no denying that.

I didn't have a hard bone in my body. Sometimes I felt like BamBam had taken all the hardness from me even before birth and had left me with all of the softness but that didn't hold up. I had eleven other siblings that were better than me as well. I was... well I was Novis.

Sometimes I believed that my life would have been more simpler if I had been born human. There had actually been a time when I had been convinced I had been a changeling but my mum would always stroke my hair with a smile and tell me I was right where I belonged.

She always believed in me, always told me to keep reading and keep discovering. I knew everything a high powered witch should, except I had no magick to back it up. Still my mum had been there for me, teaching me diligently as if it didn't matter that I could never use anything she was teaching.

I sighed, it still would have been easier to be born a human. I wouldn't have to worry about any of the magick bullshit, wouldn't have had to deal with the drama of being a witch with virtually no magick. I wouldn't have had to deal with the fact I was completely and totally inadequate. I had been expected to be amazing after BamBam had been born. I was the second eldest. I should have been just as good as BamBam or close to her power level. Instead there had been nothing.

I was a disappointment.

I was fairly certain my family wished I had been born a human too. Well mainly my father but I barely saw him anymore. He never came home and I was fairly certain he was cavorting around with his harem. I grimaced at that before my face fell as I walked towards home. I would never be married to a warlock. I was a witch with little magick, that left me to be nothing but a bed warmer. Someone a warlock could fuck but not marry. I would be part of the harems I so despised and I *hated* myself for it.

There was nothing I could do about that fate, if I wanted a warlock that would be as close as I came to one. There was no way a warlock would willingly marry me. Any child we would have would be mediocre at magick at best, completely without magick at worse. I wore Novis to keep the hurtful words at bay but being Nolo Vis was a fucking *curse.*

Just once in my life I wanted to look up and see those damned lines glow in the darkness of the room as the Divines blessed me with the power I knew I should have been born with. I wanted to see it just once because then I wouldn't feel so sick inside when I looked in the mirror. Perhaps then a warlock would see me as something of worth rather than something he could fuck and discard.

I scurried down the side of the buildings, looking for the familiar lines of my family home. "Tomorrow. I will try again tomorrow." I said it every day but that hope, that want to see it happen, kept me going back to the awakening temple to do my spell day after day. I would try and try again.

There was nothing else I *could* do.

This book recognizes the upset this publishing has caused in certain individuals in a certain group but the author of this book does not care about the upset and those individuals can suck it.

Suck it.